THE HAT,
THE UMBRELLA
AND THE LITTLE
WHITE GLOVES

CAROL PRIOR

For my brother Alan

Winchelsea Publications

CHAPTER 1

THE HAT!

I T WAS A Saturday when the hat arrived on the doorstep. Clarissa opened the front door to check the weather and she saw it there. It was silky black and shiny with a high crown and a small brim so she picked it up and admired it. Then, because it looked as if it was going to rain, she opened the gate and went out into the street and gazed in both directions to see if there was any sign of the owner.

Where had it come from? Had it blown in? she asked herself but as there was nothing further to be done she walked back up the steps and took it indoors. Once inside she put it on and looked at her reflection in the mirror on the hallstand, it fitted her well. She tried to decide what she should do with it. Was there a home for hats that were lost or unwanted? It was time for breakfast so she lifted the lid of the carved trunk that sat in the hallway and popped it in along with the boots and odd gloves that needed to be sorted. It looked a bit out of place and seemed to sulk as she closed the lid as if to say, 'I'm not accustomed to being shut away in any old trunk, I'm used to being on the stage.'

Everyone was sitting around the big table in the dining room. There were six children in all. Claudia, the eldest, who was thirteen years old, handed around the menus that they had made one wet afternoon.

'I'll have the devilled kidneys,' said Chloe, 'with the fried bread.'

Chloe, who was just nine, had long golden hair that reached down to the hem of her dress, and she was very beautiful with clear blue eyes so everyone envied her.

'I don't like the sound of that at all! I'll have the tripe,' said Clodhilde, known to all as Clod which she hated. (Father was supposed to register her as Clothilde but he had been so distracted by work that he had accidently put a 'd' where the 't' should have been.)

'Whatever that is, I don't want it,' declared Alexander, 'it sounds revolting!'

'Eggs for me,' said Clarissa, 'and I will share with baby.'

She picked up baby, also known as Antoine on the rare occasions that Mother came out of her room.

'Thank you,' said Claudia, 'now please give me back the menus.'

She left the room and returned five minutes later with a tray of rolls, then went again and came back immediately with a huge jug of hot chocolate that dripped on the floor all the way from the kitchen to the dining room and slopped on the table when she poured it.

'Oh, good, bread and jam again,' cried Clod, and she clapped her hands.

Clarissa didn't mention the hat, it was her secret. She thought about how it was snuggling down amid the odds and ends in the trunk and she knew it wasn't happy and she wondered how she would find its owner. Surely someone would be looking for it at this very moment.

Saturday was cleaning day so they finished breakfast and cleared the table and everyone scurried around with dusters and brooms. Alexander was only ten but tall for his age so his job was to stand on chairs and reach up as high as possible. It was a thankless task as the spiders saw him coming and climbed up even higher to escape his feather duster which, though it had a long handle, only reached halfway up the walls.

The old house on the Rue Gladioli was typical of Parisian houses. It had green shutters over long windows, and tall gables and a pretty metal gate decorated with copper flowers and leaves. Once it had been grand, when there were servants with ladders to chase the spiders from the ceilings and clean the long windows. Now the dining room was only swept on a Saturday so a whole colony of mice ran around the floors and could be heard at night squeaking and scampering in the walls. The old cat, Mathilde, couldn't keep up with the task of chasing and eating so many mice and they laughed at her in their squeaky voices from the doorway to the kitchen where she slept most of the day.

Mother named her Mathilde after a long dead parrot that she owned when she was in the theatre. It had been her life, the theatre not the parrot, but after the children arrived she reluctantly abandoned her acting career altogether and took to her room in the Rue Gladioli.

She filled it with posters advertising her shows, and photographs of fellow actors in their stage makeup all smiling and pulling funny faces. There was a long pink velvet chaise and matching drapes, and peacock feathers; and a rainbow of fluffy boas draped pleasingly over the bedposts. As for Father, he was seldom, if ever, seen for he was totally engrossed in his work as a financier in the Avenue Ricarde in the First Arrondissement. It was hard to decide if any of the children would even recognise him if he were to call in.

They were looked after, and I use the term loosely, by an ancient English nanny who was about ninety and answered to the name of Floss, though Claudia said she thought it was short for Florence.

Floss, or Florence, staggered around all day with the aid of a walking stick and any piece of furniture that happened to be near enough to lean upon. She laughed at their antics and wasn't at all bothered about the state of the house, or what they ate, or even whether or not they went to school.

Chaotic was the word that best described their daily lives but no one seemed to mind at all or even notice.

For the most part, Clarissa forgot about the hat in the trunk. Occasionally it came to mind but she was soon consumed by everyday clutter. She decided it must be the hat of a magician, or even the ringmaster of a circus, but still she had no idea of how to return it to its original owner. Perhaps it was left there for me on purpose, she thought but she couldn't fathom why anyone would want to leave it for her, especially as there was no attached message.

CHAPTER 2

THE UMBRELLA!

C LARISSA TOOK THE hat from the trunk on the Friday evening and tried it on again. This time she didn't recognise her face in the mirror. It had changed and she looked somehow older and not like herself at all. She took it off quickly and threw it into the carved trunk without a moment's hesitation.

'Maybe that's why someone put it on the step,' she murmured, 'they just wanted to get rid of it and they didn't care where it went.' And she was just deciding where she could leave it for the best when baby needed to be bathed and put to bed. That usually took an hour at least, what with the stories and the lullabies, by which time the hat was again forgotten.

The next day it was Chloe who opened the door to check on the weather. It was an autumn day and the chestnut tree opposite the house looked as though it was floating on the grass verge and its candlestick blossoms glowed pale and ghostly in the mist. She glanced at the tree and the blossoms and thought how beautiful they were then she noticed the umbrella at the bottom of the steps just in front of the gate. It was black and silky like the hat, with indigo metal spikes and a golden handle. It was altogether a very elegant umbrella; the golden handle had been carved into a curlicue in the shape of a dragon's head and was inscribed with the words *'To a valued friend with grateful thanks!'* Chloe didn't know about the hat that was nestling at the bottom of the trunk in the hall or she might have thought the abandoned umbrella was a sign that something very strange was going on. She picked it up and examined it, just as Clarissa had studied the hat, then she went out onto the street and stared both ways into the misty distance. No one was in sight so she went back through the gate and climbed the steps into the house. Then for no reason that she was aware of, she opened the carved trunk and, without even glancing inside, threw the umbrella into its depths and slammed the lid.

Clarissa found it on the Tuesday. She had begun to lie awake at night, often until two in the morning, while Claudia, Clod and Chloe breathed softly and murmured in their sleep and baby Antoine snuffled. Her dreams were full of the hat. It danced across in front of her and sometimes it sang strange songs, which is a very odd thing for a hat to do.

Other times she dreamt of a tall, thin man who was throwing it in the air and catching it straight onto his head. Then she would sit up wide awake with her heart pounding. It has to go, she decided, which was why she lifted the lid of the trunk on the Tuesday and found not only the hat but also the elegant umbrella.

She took the umbrella outside and opened it because she knew it was unlucky to put it up in the house, and then she twirled it by its golden dragon's head handle. Was it her imagination or did she lift just slightly off the ground. She closed it quickly and threw it onto the bottom step. 'Well I don't know where you came from,' she said out loud, 'but you, and that hat, will have to go,' and she added, 'as soon as possible!'

The door opened behind her and Claudia appeared, she was wearing the hat, it didn't quite fit over her dark brown curls.

'Where did this…' she stopped when she saw Clarissa throwing the umbrella. 'Well I was going to ask where this hat came from but there's an umbrella too!'

'Take it off,' cried Clarissa. 'It's a magic hat!' she added when she saw Claudia's alarmed face. 'I'll tell you all about how it came to be in the trunk and you can help me to decide what we should do with it. I really don't know where the umbrella came from but it will have to go as well.' And Clarissa told Claudia all about the strange dreams that had haunted her since she found the hat.

Claudia listened carefully, 'I think we should find out who put the umbrella in the trunk,' she said, 'after all, it can't have climbed in there on its own.'

A shudder ran down Clarissa's back and she shivered, 'Maybe it was trying to rescue the hat,' she murmured.

'No, umbrellas do not rescue hats,' said Claudia firmly, 'so let's ask the others which of them found it.'

'I put it in the trunk,' admitted Chloe, 'I didn't know what else to do with it but I didn't know there was a hat there too!'

'We'll put them back then,' said Claudia, 'and decide what to do next when they're safely shut away.'

That afternoon there was a storm and the leaves

began to fall from the trees. They blew hither and thither past the windows, lying in piles then rising up again with the wind, like an orange, red and yellow blizzard. The children sat in the library on an old sofa that was full of holes from where the cat had clawed it.

'Probably in search of a nest of mice that's somewhere inside,' suggested Alexander, and he laughed at the horrified look on their faces. Chloe leapt up and stared at the seat as if a giant mouse was about to appear. She flicked her golden hair back behind her shoulders and went to sit on a cushion in front of the French windows where she continued to read.

'Why don't we go out instead of sitting here?' she said after a few moments. 'We should take that horrid hat and the elegant umbrella and leave them in the park to be covered in old leaves and we'll never see them again.'

They all agreed it was an excellent idea so Claudia wrapped baby Antoine in his thick coat and woolly leggings and sat him in his perambulator. Then Alexander helped her to lift it down the stone steps and through the gate onto the pavement and they set off. Clarissa carried the hat in a big paper bag so that she wouldn't have to look at it, and Chloe and

Clodhilde carried the umbrella between them.

The park was just across from the Rue Gladioli and soon they were among the swirling leaves that lay deep on the paths, shuffling along and kicking them into the air while baby Antoine shrieked in delight. The trees loomed out of the autumn mist and the air had a crisp, leafy smell.

'We'll leave them under that tree,' said Clarissa, and she pointed to a large oak not too far from the path. Baby Antoine cooed with joy as he was bumped across the wet grass to where a pile of leaves lay against the oak. 'Just here,' said Clarissa, 'maybe they won't be found until spring comes and the park keeper will put them in the rubbish because by then no one will want them.'

'It does seem odd that someone would lose an umbrella with an inscription; not to mention the fact that it has a gold handle,' observed Alexander as they piled leaves and stray branches over them until they were completely hidden from anyone passing by.

By the time they were nearly home the rain was pounding on the pavements and streaming down the gutters while the drains gurgled with a merry, bubbling tune.

'Perhaps we should have kept the umbrella,' remarked Clod, 'after all no one else seems to want it and it is a perfect umbrella day you must agree?'

'I think we've done the right thing,' said Claudia, 'especially if it helps Clarissa to sleep at night.'

CHAPTER 3

THE LITTLE WHITE GLOVES!

AND THAT SHOULD have been that, and for a while it was. It was more than two weeks later, when the leaves were piled high in the garden and a hint of frost was in the air, that Clarissa stepped out of the front door on the Saturday morning to check on the weather. It was very cold and she could see her breath in the chill air and, lying on the ground in front of the gate, two tiny white gloves.

'I mustn't panic,' she told herself. 'I'm sure they belong to a child who has lost them and if I leave them on the wall someone is certain to stop by and find them.' Then she went indoors and told the others about the white gloves.

'It's rather a coincidence,' said Clod. 'Why is it always our doorstep? It's not as if there aren't people living next door. I suspect there is a reason why we are being chosen.' Then she went outside and took them down from the wall. 'There's no name or label,' she announced from the doorway, 'not a single clue as to the owner of these gloves,' she pulled them on, 'but they fit me perfectly!' She carried them indoors and put them in the carved trunk in the hall ready for when winter came and it was really cold. After that she closed the lid and went off to read as it was a Saturday and therefore there was nothing else to do but the weekly clean and she preferred to avoid that.

However, inside the trunk something very remarkable was happening. All the odd gloves had somehow found each other and rolled themselves into little woolly balls, and the boots had lined themselves up in the bottom making lots of room for any more objects that might turn up on the doorstep. Anyone who looked into the trunk would have realised immediately that something extraordinary was going on. Maybe some magic had spilled out of the black hat and been left behind before it was taken to the park and abandoned along with the umbrella. Or perhaps it was something to do with the white gloves being very bossy. If so it would have been quite useful to take them out just to see if they could organise the house as efficiently because the chaos had spread.

Now Floss spent most of the day lounging in a battered old patchwork chair by the fire and she never checked to see if the children had cleaned their teeth, or if they changed their socks. Luckily Claudia had taken control of most things. They had given up visiting their Mother; she never seemed interested in anything they did in any case though they often heard her at night when they were tucked up in their beds. She would wander down to the kitchen and raid the cupboards for food and carry it back upstairs to her room. Or sometimes they would hear her singing melancholy songs from her old life on the stage as she drifted ghost-like around the house.

'We really should do something about Mother,' said Clarissa to Alexander. He had moved into their room and slept on a mattress on the floor which was better, he said, 'than being in a draughty house with the wind whistling around the chimneys and a weird woman that no one ever saw.'

'And, it's fortunate that we get our groceries delivered,' she added, 'or we would all starve.'

'Maybe she's not our Mother at all,' he said, 'perhaps our Mother has been taken away by fairies and this one is a replacement.'

'They're called changelings,' said Clarissa 'but I don't think it's happened to Mother. No, I believe she's just very sad because she misses her life in the theatre with all the glitz and excitement. And maybe, just maybe, she misses Papa a little.'

Then they went to sleep.

CHAPTER 4

THE WHITE RABBIT

LIFE WENT ON as usual in the big old house on the Rue Gladioli. Winter came and snow piled up against the windows blocking out the draughts, which was lucky because they had very little coal left for the fire; and food had to be rationed as the delivery truck couldn't get through the snow for almost a week.

The colony of mice had increased greatly as Mathilde had decided to join Floss on the old patchwork chair and she rarely moved, apart from when she got up to go to bed. More than once they wondered if Mathilde was still alive, and Chloe, who was very kind hearted, said that they should check to see if Floss was still breathing on several occasions.

Spring came at last. Clarissa looked out of their bedroom window one morning and noticed a solitary daffodil poking through the damp earth and she felt really happy. Then she went downstairs to open the front door and breathe the fresh spring air. It was when she walked through the hall that she heard an odd sound, a kind of scraping noise that seemed to be coming from inside the carved trunk, so she turned back with a worried expression on her face.

'Oh no,' she murmured, 'the wretched mice have invaded the trunk!' She lifted the lid cautiously, just a crack, for she wasn't keen on mice, and a small nose poked through at her. It was a pink nose with whiskers and little pink eyes.

'It's a white rabbit!' she shrieked. 'How did it get in there?'

Everyone came running when they heard her scream and they all gasped in amazement at the furry creature that lay in Clarissa's arms.

'It's very sweet,' said Claudia, and baby Antoine, who was clasping her tight around the neck, reached out to stroke it.

It was then that they noticed the gloves and boots that no one had bothered to wear anyway, even in the snow.

'Who has tidied the boots and put the gloves into pairs?' asked Clod. She took out the white gloves and put them on, 'Oh I'd quite forgotten about these,' she added.

Then Chloe opened the door to check the weather and there at the bottom of the steps, just inside the gate, was the black hat and right next to it, the elegant umbrella.

They looked in perfect condition, untouched by the rain and snow and without a trace of dust or grime from being buried beneath the leaves. She stood in shocked silence gazing down on them and when she didn't return the others came out and they all stood in complete silence and stared at the black hat and the elegant umbrella (with the indigo metal spikes, the inscription, and the golden curlicue handle in the shape of a dragon's head).

'What are we to do?' said Clarissa at last.

She sighed deeply and the rabbit looked up at her and twitched its whiskers as if to say, 'It's nothing to do with me, I am only a rabbit and I am as baffled as you are.'

Clod waved her white gloved hands in the air and exclaimed very dramatically, which wasn't like her at all in the normal way, 'We must bring them inside and put them back in the trunk until we think of another plan!' Then she looked down at the white gloves anxiously and wondered why her hands were tingling, almost as if small bolts of electricity were shooting through her fingers and out of the ends of her fingernails into the air around.

'But where have they come from?' asked Claudia. 'We hid them under the leaves in the park ages ago. They should definitely have rotted away by now yet they're as immaculate as ever they were before, and there's not the slightest sign of rust on the spokes of the umbrella.'

'Indestructible!' muttered Alexander. He walked down the steps very calmly and picked up the hat in one hand and the umbrella in the other and brought them back to where the others stood in a huddle in the doorway.

Clarissa recoiled, 'Take them away,' she cried, 'that horrible hat frightens me more than I can say!' and she thrust the startled white rabbit at Chloe who only just managed to catch it. Then she marched off to the library in floods of tears and locked herself in.

Alexander opened the trunk and put the hat and the umbrella inside, and then he banged the lid shut and rushed after Clarissa. He came back a few moments later, 'She's locked the door, what should we do next?'

'Hush...' murmured Claudia to baby Antoine

who had started to bawl, 'Let's sit on the steps and make a plan before Floss wakes up to see what all the fuss is.'

Clod pulled off the white gloves and dropped them on the floor then she went outside to sit on the top step nearest the door. She could still hear Clarissa's sobs echoing around the house so she got up and moved nearer to the gate.

'As I see it,' said Alexander from the next step up, 'we have no choice but to find a way to get rid of them completely, otherwise we'll never get back in the library again. And actually that is quite important since we never go to school.'

They all nodded in agreement and were just debating various ways of disposing of the hat and umbrella for good when a gust of wind came from nowhere and slammed the front door shut with an enormous bang. The white rabbit jumped violently and leapt out of Chloe's arms. It ran down the steps and across the road in the direction of the park just as the baker's van came tearing around the bend. Chloe screamed and covered her eyes.

'It's alright, you can look now,' said Alexander. 'Bobtail made it to the park and I think that's the best place for it!'

'But how are we going to get in?' wailed Clod.

'We can't rely on Floss or Mother to open the door. There's only Clarissa and she's trapped in there with the hat, the umbrella and the white gloves!'

'If you ask me,' said Chloe, 'it was the hat that slammed the door!'

They all stared at her, 'Do you really think so?' asked Claudia, who was holding baby Antoine as tight as she could as he was trying to wriggle off after the rabbit.

'Yes, I really do,' said Chloe, 'I think the hat is a magic one, and the umbrella, and the gloves. They're all magic and if we want to get them out of our lives forever we will have to be even more clever and powerful than they are.'

Clarissa had stopped crying now so they knocked on the door and she came to let them in; her eyes were red and her face was stained with tears. 'It was the hat' she said, 'that slammed the door but you've guessed that, haven't you?'

She went to the trunk and opened it and took out the hat and the umbrella then she walked calmly down the steps and threw them into the middle of the road.

'The baker's van has already been,' said Clod helpfully; 'but I'm sure there'll be other reckless drivers,' she added when Claudia glared at her.

CHAPTER 5

WHERE ARE THE WHITE GLOVES?

THE LIBRARY FELT safe somehow as if untouched by the goings on in the rest of the house. It had three walls of shelves all crammed with books of every kind. There were small books on the top shelves that were old, and smelled of mildew, but further down were larger books with pictures and diagrams full of useful information. The fourth wall was mainly glass with French windows that opened out into a large shady garden. No one went into the garden these days. At one time, when Claudia and Clarissa were small, it was full of flowers, and gardeners came at least twice a week to pull out the weeds and cut the grass. They could remember their Mother and Father sitting outside on deckchairs laughing and joking with friends, and having tea on the lawn. In those days they were Mama and Papa and everyone was happy.

Clarissa wasn't sure what went wrong, only that things seemed to change gradually without anyone appearing to notice and now their lives were completely different. She picked up baby Antoine and he giggled and pulled her hair.

'Let's write a list of possibilities,' said Claudia, 'who's got some paper, and a pen?'

Alexander jumped up from the old sofa that was full of holes, 'They're in the desk. I'll get them.'

He opened the drawer of the desk, which was a very old antique dating from the time of Napoleon (according to Floss in one of her more lucid moments), then came back and gave Claudia two sheets of paper and a pencil.

'Now,' she said, 'what can we do to dispose of the hat and the umbrella?' And she wrote a number '1' in the margin.

'Don't forget the gloves!' cried Clod. She remembered with a jolt that she had dropped them on the floor in the hall and decided that as soon as possible they must be thrown into the road too.

'And the gloves,' continued Claudia, and she added, 'of course the hat and the umbrella might be completely squashed already in which case there's no need for us to do anything, and we can always burn the gloves.'

When she said this, Clod was certain that she heard a howl from the direction of the hall and she glanced around waiting for someone to mention it but no one did. In fact, everyone looked relieved except Clarissa; she knew somehow that the hat and the umbrella were indestructible as Alexander had said. How else could they be in such perfect condition after spending a cold winter buried under an oak tree in the park?

'We could just put them back in the carved trunk in the hall,' suggested Alexander and Clarissa's mouth dropped open in horror.

'How can you be so mean!' she asked sadly.

'Of course, it would need a strong padlock so they couldn't ever get out,' continued Alexander.

'Please don't put that on the list,' pleaded Clarissa, 'I wouldn't get a moment's sleep knowing they were down there in the trunk in the hall!'

'Fine,' he went on, 'but actually the only problem so far is you having a few bad dreams. I know they came back from the park though, which I suppose is a bit odd, and there's the slammed door, but that could have been the wind.'

Claudia had been writing a list of her own, 'Listen,' she said, 'this is my list. Pass it round and add anything you like. Providing it's sensible,' and she glared at Alexander who shuffled uncomfortably and looked down at the moth-eaten rug by his feet.

'I'll read it out,' said Chloe,

'1. Bury them in the park again but this time further away.
2. Leave in the market place and hope that someone steals them.
3. Sell to an antique dealer.
4. Leave them on a bus or a train.
5. Find the owner of the elegant umbrella with the inscription and hope that he knows who owns the black hat and white gloves.
6. Tell Mother, or Floss, and ask for help.'

She looked up and grinned at Claudia, 'Brilliant, I'm sure one of those will work, well, all but the last one!'

'Oh, we forgot to have breakfast!' Clod exclaimed suddenly, 'Where are the menus?'

And she hurried out into the hall to look for the white gloves while the others made the breakfast which this time was eggs, bacon and mushrooms all round but, as usual, came out looking like bread and jam.

Clod searched in vain for the white gloves but she couldn't find them anywhere and in the end she decided it would be much safer not to mention them again.

CHAPTER 6

CAKE!

NO ONE LEFT the house that day; they were all too afraid that the hat and the umbrella might be back and then Clarissa would have another fit of hysterics. To make matters worse there had been very little traffic along the road so it seemed unlikely that the hat would be squashed, at least until the baker's van came back.

The next morning the room was full of bright sunlight that fell on their faces as the curtains had become so thin. Clarissa lay in bed trying to decide whether she should open the front door. She was fairly certain that the top hat and umbrella would be waiting on the step ready to terrorise her further but she knew someone would have to open it, sooner or later.

She could hear shouts from downstairs in the kitchen and wondered if Mathilde, or perhaps even Floss, had passed away in the night so she jumped quickly out of bed and ran down to see what the hullaballoo was all about. Floss was still alive, as was the cat, but both were slumped as usual, Mathilde in front of the fireplace and Floss in her patchwork chair by the stove. She was fast asleep and snoring; her neck wobbled every time she took a breath and her arms were flung back over the chair arms so she looked like a very fat pigeon about to take off. Well that's alright, thought Clarissa then she turned to where everyone else was crowded around the kitchen table. In the middle was a large cake, it had white and pink icing and on the top were a snowman, a Christmas tree, and a little sign that said 'Merry Christmas One and All'.

'Where did that come from?' she gasped, 'it's lovely!'

'It's a fruit cake with marzipan and there's a note on it,' said Chloe, and she flicked her golden hair behind her ears so that she could see to read. 'Look, it says, 'For the children who didn't have a Christmas' and there are six kisses on the bottom!'

Clarissa glanced at her brothers and sisters. Their eyes were shining and baby Antoine was already holding a lump of icing that Claudia had broken off for him.

'Do you think Floss made it?' asked Clod, 'Maybe that's why she's even more tired than usual?'

'Is that possible?' asked Alexander, 'Oh well, I don't care who made it, I know what I'm having for breakfast!' He picked up the plate with the cake on it and carried it into the dining room while Clarissa collected the plates and mugs and Chloe made a jug of hot chocolate.

Clod hung back for she had seen something that made her heart sink. Just under the patchwork chair was a white glove. She picked it up and noted that it was dusty with icing sugar and slightly sticky and buttery. The other glove was nowhere to be seen so she shrugged and put it down next to the stove that was still warm. 'Well, we know it was baked here,' she said to herself, and she went off to join the others.

It was a glorious cake they decided. They weren't quite sure if glorious was a word that could be used for cake but it sounded right and it was big enough for two breakfasts, or possibly even three.

'A sponge with strawberry jam would be nice for tea,' mumbled Alexander as he stuffed a glazed cherry into his mouth even though it was already full of icing and sultanas. 'Perhaps Mother came down in the night and made it? And maybe she's going to cook all our food from now on?'

'Has anyone checked the weather this morning?' Clod asked.

'I think it's going to be a beautiful day,' said Claudia, 'but we have to make sure that both the hat and the umbrella have been squashed so maybe we should wait until the baker's van has been. Let's have some more cake and then check on the weather. We'll wait until the clock strikes ten.'

When ten o'clock came it was Claudia who went to open the door while the others waited in the hall outside the kitchen. Clarissa sat in the dining room with her hands pressed firmly over her ears. She was waiting for Claudia's scream. She was absolutely sure that there would be a scream even though the baker's boy had raced past the house at half past nine only stopping to throw two crusty white baguettes onto the step. It would have been too much to hope that the hat and the umbrella were directly in line with the wheels and if they were wouldn't he do his very best to avoid them? He might spot them and think, what a lovely black hat, and what an elegant umbrella and perhaps even stop and pick them up off the road to keep for himself, but she knew somehow that she would be wrong. Her worst fears were realised when she heard a loud shriek from the hallway.

'They're back!' wailed Claudia, 'Look, they're right outside the door this time! How is that possible?'

Clarissa rushed out of the dining room to join the others in the hall. She was overcome with hatred for the hat.

'Where is it?' she cried angrily, and, 'Oh, no!' when she saw it leaning over the step next to the bread as if waiting for the door to open so that it could hop inside.

The umbrella was there too, resting against the newel post in a jaunty fashion almost as if it were saying, 'Hey, we're back, aren't you pleased to see us?'

Clarissa burst into tears and turned and dashed down the hallway. They heard the library door slam behind her.

'She's done it again,' Alexander said in a bored voice.

'So, what next?' asked Chloe, 'Things can't go on like this, can they?'

'It's time for the list,' said Claudia solemnly, 'and we left it in the library but maybe Clarissa will let us in if she knows that we mean to deal with the problem straight away!'

Clod tapped gently on the library door, 'Clarissa, dear, please let us in. We know how upset you are and we're going to do something about it. We have to have the list though and it's on the antique desk. Please come out!'

The library door opened just a crack and Clarissa peered around the door at Clod who could see only one large grey eye and an auburn curl on a pale cheek. Clarissa posted the list through the narrow gap and slammed the door again almost catching Clod on the nose. Clod leapt back just in time, then she picked up the list that had fallen on the floor and took it back to the others.

'What now?' Alexander asked.

'Back to the dining room,' said Chloe.

'Oh no!' cried Clod when they opened the door, 'the mice! We forgot to put the cake in the larder!'

The cake could hardly be seen for mice. They were wriggling and running, and fighting over every crumb, all nibbling and squealing with delight. Claudia shut the door, she was almost in tears, 'It was such a glorious cake,' she murmured.

'Huh, the dining room, and the library are out of bounds now!' exclaimed Alexander, 'let's try the kitchen.'

'How can we decide anything in the kitchen?' asked Clod, 'Floss and Mathilde are snoring and anyway there's nowhere for us all to sit, is there?'

'It will have to be the front parlour then,' said Claudia gloomily.

The front parlour was large and cold with hard furniture and no cushions. There was a giant sideboard covered in ancient photographs of grim looking relations named Hortense and Bernard and suchlike, and faded Turkish carpets that were scattered around the floor. In one corner stood an Aspidistra in a china pot; it had once been tall with glossy green leaves but was now shrivelled and brown because no one bothered to water it.

Chloe walked to the window and looked out on the street. She could just see the brim of the black hat as it sat on the step. 'Why won't it leave us alone,' she murmured, 'whoever would have thought that a hat could be so sinister?'

She pulled the curtains across and turned back to the others, 'We should take it back to the park along with that umbrella, and bury them, except this time we should dig a deep hole and fill it in and then cover the whole lot with a big rock!'

If they had seen the hat at this moment they would have realised how angry it was at this suggestion. It tapped at the door violently with its small brim then turned its crown to the door as if it was listening for further suggestions as to its fate.

'Tsk, tsk,' muttered the umbrella and it rattled its indigo spikes and poked the hat with its spiky end. The hat rolled to the bottom of the steps and glared back malevolently, though that was only evident to the umbrella, and it spread itself out to take up most of the top step so that there was no longer any room for the hat.

The library door was flung shut with a loud bang and Clarissa's footsteps echoed down the hall. 'I refuse to let that horrible hat get the better of me,' she cried as she burst into the front parlour, 'I am angrier than I can possibly say and I have an idea!'

Everyone sat in silence as Clarissa explained her plan, all the while pacing up and down the room with a determined frown on her face.

'It's very simple! All we have to do is take it, and the umbrella, to the Lost Property Office at the station. We can say that we found them on the bus.' She looked around at the others and waited for their reaction.

'It seems like a good solution,' said Clod eventually, 'it would certainly save all that digging and lugging rocks about, and that suits me. Plus, the Lost Property Office is further away so it would take years for them to get back here.'

'Yes,' said Claudia, 'we should give it a try but we'll have to go straight away because not many buses go all the way to the station and it's already nearly time for lunch.'

Alexander sighed mournfully, 'And I was really looking forward to cake for lunch.'

'Let's fetch the bread from the step and take it on the bus. It will be just like a picnic,' said Claudia. 'Now who is willing to catch the hat?'

'I am not afraid of a hat,' declared Alexander, 'at least hats don't eat cake, unlike those revolting mice!'

CHAPTER 7

LE PERROQUET!

'WHAT'S THAT PECULIAR noise?' asked Alexander when they were back in the hall.

'Just Floss,' said Clod, 'she's snoring and it's so loud that it makes the saucepans rattle. I don't know how Mathilde manages to sleep at all!'

'We know Floss snores, Clod, but listen, what is that scrabbling noise coming from the trunk?'

'I can hear it too,' said Chloe, 'it sounds like…'

'Mice,' cried Clod, 'please don't open it.'

'I don't see how mice could have got inside the trunk,' Chloe said and she flung open the lid.

'Rabbits!' yelled Claudia.

'Wabbits!' shouted baby Antoine when about twenty white rabbits with pink noses and twitching whiskers leapt out of the trunk and headed for the front door.

'Open the door,' yelled Chloe to Clarissa who

was standing next to it in case she needed to escape in a hurry. The rabbits fled down the steps jumping over the umbrella and scattering the bread. They ran over the silky black hat covering it in dusty footprints, then through the copper metal leaves of the gate and across the road, narrowly avoiding the grocer's van.

'The bus goes very soon,' declared Claudia in a matter of fact voice as if she had become accustomed to odd events, 'we should hurry or we'll miss it.'

Alexander picked up the hat from the bottom step, where it had landed when the umbrella pushed it, and placed it carefully in an old hat box that Clarissa found in a wardrobe. Next they wrapped the umbrella in brown paper and set off for the bus stop. No one mentioned the white gloves at all.

The bus soon came rattling along the road. It was a big yellow bus with an upstairs that meant they could look down on all the gardens as they went along. They climbed the narrow curved steps and made for the front seats; baby Antoine sat on Claudia's knee next to Alexander who held the hat box, while Chloe, who was carrying the umbrella, shared a seat on the other side with Clod and Clarissa. The bus sailed along past the park and the boating lake which looked blue and sparkling in the sunshine but there were no toy boats because it was a school day.

Every now and then it stopped for ladies with shopping baskets who were laughing and joking with each other, or men in suits with hats and brief cases. The streets gradually became busier and the traffic slowed them down but soon the conductor shouted, 'Station, next stop,' so they clambered down the steps and waited on the bus platform for it to come to a halt.

There were cafes everywhere, all with bright stripy awnings and umbrellas, and tables spilling out onto the streets. The aroma of fresh coffee and cooking food wafted under Alexander's nose making his mouth water. It all looked delicious and inviting; he licked his lips and felt his stomach rumble.

'Keep up, Alexander,' called Claudia impatiently when he stopped to press his face against the window of one of the little cafes. A waiter with a moustache glared at him from behind the counter and he glared back and put out his tongue making a damp mark on the glass. Then he stopped for a moment and looked around carefully to see if anyone was watching; no one seemed to be so he put the hat box down next to the wall and ran after Claudia who was shepherding everyone across the road.

'You've forgotten your hat!' called a gruff voice. He tried to ignore it but the waiter with the moustache wasn't about to give up, 'Boy, come back. You left your hat behind!'

Alexander considered whether or not to make a run for it but the waiter was moving quickly towards him between the tables and chairs.

'Your mother wouldn't thank you if you lost her hat,' he said.

Alexander took it reluctantly and thanked him because he had always been taught to be polite.

He crossed the road to join the others. Cars and buses were racing towards him from every direction and a policeman with a whistle was trying to direct the traffic. They went inside; it seemed even noisier and more bustling and there was the roar of trains puffing in and out of the station and a smell that was a bit like eggs that had boiled for too long. Chloe held her nose, and Clod put her fingers in her ears; baby Antoine just stared around taking everything in with wide blue eyes and an open mouth.

'We have to go this way,' shouted Clarissa above the din, and she pointed to a sign that said 'Lost Property Office' in big red and gold letters.

'Oh very nice!' gushed the man behind the desk, 'You found them on a bus, you say? Take a look at this George, it says, 'to a valued friend with grateful thanks', you'd think he would have looked after it better. I know lots of people who would like these; lovely hat, ain't it, George?'

'Gone!' cried Clarissa when they were back in the station, and she did a little dance just to show how glad she was.

'Stop,' said Alexander, 'or people will start throwing money.'

'We can always hope,' said Clod, 'we only just managed to scrape enough together for our bus fare!'

Clarissa laughed happily, 'Anyway, we should celebrate now that the hat has gone; at last!'

'Actually, I thought the umbrella was rather nice,' remarked Chloe 'and it was always the hat that you disliked so much. Still it wasn't our umbrella so we did the right thing by handing it in.'

They could see the windmill sails of the Moulin Rouge as they wandered up the narrow streets to where the beautiful white Cathedral gleamed at the very top of the hill.

'It's like a giant cake,' said Claudia, and she put baby Antoine down because the hill was steep and he toddled along next to her.

'It's not as nice as our cake,' sighed Alexander, 'the one that the mice ate. I wonder who made it.'

'It must have been Floss,' said Clarissa. 'Mother hasn't been out of her room in years, at least during the daytime.'

'Maybe she's become nocturnal,' suggested Clod, 'like a bat, or one of those odd monkeys with the giant eyes.' (She had been reading lots of books about strange and exotic animals, mainly to avoid the Saturday house clean).

'I know Mother is rather strange,' said Chloe, 'but I don't think you should compare her to a monkey, after all, she's still our Mother, even if we never see her!'

Soon they came to a leafy square where artists had set up their easels in puddles of warm sunshine.

'Portraits?' called a young man with a tiny beard in the middle of his chin; he beckoned to Chloe and she backed away.

'No charge, Mademoiselle, you have such beautiful hair.'

Clod looked sulky, 'It's not fair; no one ever likes my hair!'

'How do you do, Mademoiselle,' he put down his charcoal and held out his hand to Clod, 'my name is Pierre and I think you have lovely hair too; it reminds me of sunflowers. I would like to draw both of you and when I am famous you will be in a grand gallery.'

Clod sat impatiently while he sketched, she was beginning to wish that she hadn't complained. She was longing to get up and dance around which was mainly because she had been told to sit still, but Chloe posed perfectly, resting her tilted chin gracefully on one hand. Eventually Pierre lifted his drawing from the easel and held it up to show them. He had captured the light shining gold through Chloe's hair, and the way it swished like a horse's tail when she flicked it behind her ears and the breeze caught it, but Clod's smile was angelic so she was happy too.

It was already getting quite late when they decided it was time to go home and they were just walking back towards the bus stop when Alexander suddenly yelled, 'Look everyone, it's the theatre where Mother used to sing on the stage, 'Le Perroquet'! We can't go home without visiting it!'

CHAPTER 8

HIRONDELLE AND MIMZI MAI

THE THEATRE HAD shallow steps leading down on the street and the front was beautifully decorated with birds and flowers made of marble. Either side of the doors there were posters, and programs about the latest acts, and pictures of the performers in elaborate costumes. They climbed the steps and pushed through the glass doors into a plush foyer with red velvet carpet.

'It is quite beautiful,' exclaimed Clarissa as she gazed around, 'so maybe I can understand why Mother was sad to leave it all behind.'

'I think it's rather insulting,' declared Clod crossly, 'I'm sure we're just as interesting and beautiful as this.'

'I'm sure you are,' said a voice. 'I remember your Mother well and I'm certain she cares for you far more than she cares for this theatre.'

They looked around to see where the voice was coming from. Standing just at the top of a flight of stairs, where the doors opened into the auditorium, stood a small woman. She was young and had a very pretty face with expressive dark brown eyes and a mop of black hair that cascaded down her back in glossy curls.

'I'm Hirondelle, come in and meet the others. I'll show you around, then maybe you'll understand why we all love this place so much.'

She took baby Antoine's hand, and Clod's, and led them through the doors into the darkness of the auditorium. It was early so the seats were empty but in the distance, on the front of a small stage, several performers were talking in an animated fashion, though their exact conversation couldn't be heard.

'Who have you got there this time, Miss Hirondelle?' asked a gentleman in a black dress suit, and he laughed.

He has a very handsome face, thought Claudia, especially when he smiles.

'They're Serafina's little ones,' said Hirondelle, 'aren't they lovely? And just like her.'

'I was never lucky enough to meet her,' said Albert, for that was his name, 'she left before I joined your merry band.'

And so charming too, thought Claudia.

'What are your names?' he asked and they told him. Clod explained that really she was Clodhilde, and about the mix up and how she should have been Clothilde.

'But then you would have been Clot for short,' said someone, who she soon discovered was Louisa, 'and Clot is far worse than Clod!' and everyone laughed which didn't please Clod very much and she decided to change it to something much nicer as soon as she possibly could.

Albert was the House Manager, he performed but also organised the show and introduced all the acts before they came on stage. There were two girls, Louisa and Francesca; they were dancers as well as singers, and Hirondelle, who was the principal singer, and Gerard, a ventriloquist with a puppet called Archie.

'I'm pleased to make your acquaintance,' said Archie which everyone found very strange especially as Gerard hardly said a thing.

Then there was a magician called Salaam with a pretty assistant called Mimzi Mai, and finally Coco, the acrobat.

Coco was the strangest person they had ever seen. Alexander described him afterwards as small and bendy. He had a huge smile that seemed to take up most of his face when he grinned. His head was shaved completely bald like a large egg and he kept cart-wheeling around the stage so it was hard to have any sort of a conversation.

'Will you stay for the show?' asked Mimzi Mai, 'it's really very good!'

'We would love to,' said Clarissa, 'but we can't miss the last bus.'

'You can stay with me,' said Mimzi Mai. 'I have a lovely apartment up on the hill. It has views over Paris. I can even see the Eifel Tower from my window.'

'You're very kind but we really need to leave now,' Claudia took baby Antoine's hand; 'if we don't then we won't get home tonight and we might be missed.'

After that everyone came outside and waved and shouted goodbye as they set off down the street to where the bus stopped.

Then they waited and waited, for an hour,

and then another hour until the lights came on and crowds filled the cafes and bars.

'It's no good,' said Chloe at last, 'it's quite evident that we have missed the last bus. We should never have gone to the theatre! What do we do now? We can't stay out all night, can we? Do you think they would let us sleep in the station?'

Claudia got up from where she had been sitting on the hard pavement with baby Antoine asleep in her arms.

'We have to go back to the theatre. Mimzi said we could stay with her and we probably won't be missed at home.'

'I feel rather awkward having to go back to the theatre,' said Clarissa, 'after they came out to wave and made such a fuss. Still, it doesn't look as if there is a choice, does it?'

'It was odd hearing Mother called Serafina,' said Alexander.

CHAPTER 9

ARCHIE

MIMZI MAI WAS in the foyer. She ran to them as soon as they came through the glass doors and lifted baby Antoine from Claudia's arms which was fortunate as she was starting to get pins and needles after holding him for so long. Then they were ushered back into the theatre.

'We have to do a show soon,' she told them, 'but you are welcome to watch and then come home with me; you can catch a bus in the morning.'

They had the best seats right in front of the stage and soon the spectators began to arrive and the theatre was full of murmuring voices and expectation. Eventually the lights were dimmed and the curtains opened to reveal an amazing sight. The scenery depicted a seaside with brightly coloured beach huts, and foamy waves, and a Punch and Judy show that looked so lifelike that it felt as though the figures could jump out of the painted backdrop at any moment. The actors were all in costume wearing striped bathing-suits and standing perfectly still to form a seaside tableau. Then the individual acts began, the singers, and dancers, and Coco the amazing acrobat. Gerard, with his dummy Archie, got the most laughs but best of all the audience liked Salaam, the Magician who produced doves from his sleeves and rabbits from his hat.

'Our trunk in the hall is much better at making rabbits,' whispered Alexander, 'we've had at least twenty and they've appeared out of nowhere! No doves though.'

Clarissa shuddered, she had quite forgotten about the rabbits, and the hat, for the moment at least.

When the curtain came down the audience stood and cheered so there were several encores of popular songs and everyone sang along with gusto.

'Did you know my Mother?' Clod asked Mimzi when they met up in the foyer to say goodbye to everyone.

'Only for a very short while,' said Mimzi, 'I replaced Lisa after…' she stopped when she saw Hirondelle put a finger to her lips.

'After what?' asked Alexander.

'After the terrible accident,' muttered Archie in his peculiar, unearthly voice. His mouth opened and shut and his black eyes swivelled around at everyone.

'Stop!' cried Gerard the Ventriloquist, and he clasped the puppet's mouth shut with his fist but Archie pulled free, 'he was a wicked magician was Marvello…'

'Stop, I said, STOP…!' screamed Gerard and he shook Archie so that his head wobbled.

'Accident, what accident, and why did you say he was a wicked magician?' asked Chloe.

'Nothing for you to worry about,' said Hirondelle, 'just an unfortunate incident that caused the magician before Salaam to leave the company. His name was Marvello, and Lisa was his assistant. But now we have the magnificent, the incomparable, Salaam and his glamorous assistant, Mimzi Mai!'

'Tell me what happened to Lisa,' demanded Clod, and she turned towards where Gerard had been sitting with Archie on his knee, but they had gone.

'As Hirondelle said, it's nothing for you to worry about,' said Albert the House Manager. 'These things happen in the theatre, it's the thrill of it all; the laughter, the gaiety, emotions run high, and egos are fragile.'

Mimzi laughed, 'That's very true! Now we must leave, it's getting late and a long way past your bedtime I'm quite sure.'

'Actually, we don't have a bedtime,' announced Clod, 'we just go to bed when we feel like it.'

They all said goodbye again and thanked everyone, and Albert told them that they must come back soon. The air was cool and the sky was full of stars when they climbed the hill and pushed their way through the crowds who laughed and called to each other as they spilled out of the little cafes. There was the sound of someone singing and a piano; and an old man playing an accordion in a pretty square. Mimzi's little apartment was right at the top of a very old house and when they looked out of the window they could see the iron railings of a small balcony and the whole of Paris spread out before them. It shone with twinkling lights, and in the distance, as Mimzi had promised, was the Eifel Tower.

Everyone was soon asleep, apart from Clarissa. She was wondering what had happened to Marvello's assistant Lisa. After a while she got up from her pile of cushions on the floor and went over to where Mimzi lay in bed. Clod was on one side and baby Antoine on the other; Alexander was sprawled across the bottom with his thumb in his mouth.

'Are you awake, Mimzi?' she asked.

'Shhhh, yes, just about,' answered Mimzi, 'is something wrong?'

'No it's all lovely, and thank you so much for letting us stay here.'

She hesitated, 'I just want to know what happened to Lisa, will you tell me, please?'

Mimzi sat up being very careful not to wake Clod and baby Antoine. 'Clarissa, kind Clarissa, as I said, I wasn't here so I can't tell you anything about it. All I do know is that…'

'Please, go on, tell me what you do know,' urged Clarissa.

'The ventriloquist, Gerard, told me that Marvello was deeply in love with your Mother, Serafina, and that he would do anything to make her his own. Lisa was very young but she was already his wife and that made it rather difficult, and your Mother didn't like Marvello at all; she thought he was very unkind to Lisa. That's why Serafina left, and, of course, because she wanted a family. I can't tell you any more, you have to go to sleep now if you want to catch the early bus tomorrow morning.'

Clarissa tiptoed back to her bed on the floor. There are more questions than answers, she thought; and I wonder if it has anything to do with the sinister black hat?

Baby Antoine woke first the next morning. He sat up and threw himself across Mimzi and Clod so that he could reach Claudia. The room was still dim but the sun was just rising and there was a rosy glow that lit up the horizon and the skeletal shape of the Eifel Tower in the distance.

Outside a man was sweeping the pavement with a big broom and it was very quiet apart from the sound of the broom scratching on the dusty cobbles.

They hurried down to the bus stop and didn't have long to wait before the bus came and they climbed aboard. It was almost empty; just a few seats were filled with people heading for work; they laughed and exchanged jokes with the conductor as it crawled and swerved slowly towards the outskirts of the city, stopping now and then to let people on and off.

Clarissa watched from the window afraid that they might miss their stop but soon Alexander gave a yell.

'It's the boating lake in the park. We have to get off!'

CHAPTER 10

CAKES AND PIES AND FAIRY CAKES!

T HE HOUSE ON the Rue Gladioli looked exactly as it had when they left except the gate was open because the baker's boy had already been. Two crusty, white baguettes leaned against the step but there was no sign at all of the black hat and the elegant umbrella. Alexander grabbed the bread and straight away bit off the crusty end. Claudia frowned at this but he just grinned back and bit off some more, then she unlocked the door and they went in.

Clarissa was more overjoyed than she could say. The hat and the umbrella had gone for good and this is where the story should have ended but unfortunately it was no ordinary hat, and no ordinary umbrella. And, as they were soon to discover, the little white gloves were anything but ordinary.

Clod ran straight to the dining room just in case

the mice had left a morsel or two of cake, though I'm sure she wouldn't have eaten it even if they had. But there was no cause for concern as not a crumb remained. The mice had even licked the plate, and one was lying on the floor next to its hole because it was too fat to crawl inside!

There were no anxious faces waiting at the window, and no one crying for missing children; in fact, nobody seemed to have noticed at all. The library looked dustier than ever, and the first thing they saw when they went into the kitchen was Floss slumped in her threadbare, patchwork chair. As usual, she was sound asleep and snoring. She looked more exhausted than ever and so did Mathilde who was sitting in front of the cold stove. The old cat stirred when they walked in and opened one eye but quickly closed it again and began to purr softly in its sleep. The stove had gone out, and the fire, which was lucky as a large pan had boiled dry and the kitchen was full of the acrid smell of burnt potatoes.

Both the white gloves were hanging from a washing line above the empty fireplace. They seemed to twitch excitedly when Clod opened the larder door.

'Look everyone,' she screamed, 'no wonder

Floss is asleep, she's baked at least three cakes and a pie, I think it's gooseberry; and little fairy cakes with pink icing!'

'Quick, close the door,' shouted Alexander, 'or the mice will find out!'

'I know you can't hear us, Floss,' murmured Claudia, 'but thank you so much. You must have worked really hard!'

'Yes, thank you, Floss,' said Clarissa and Chloe.

'We're sorry we didn't come home last night,' added Clarissa, 'I hope you weren't worried.'

'I'll never leave home again if she keeps this up,' said Alexander, and he stuffed a whole fairy cake into his mouth.

Only Chloe gazed suspiciously at the gloves. She was sure that one tiny white finger had pointed at the larder while the other glove did a little dance. Then she decided that if they were magic too it was the kind of magic she could live with quite happily.

CHAPTER 11

CLARISSA'S BIRTHDAY

T HE MONTHS PASSED quickly and soon it was
May. Clarissa had her twelfth birthday on
the first Sunday of the month and they got up
to find a delicious chocolate sponge in the larder
complete with twelve candles. She couldn't
remember having a birthday cake for many
years and they all started speculating on what
kind of cake would appear for Clod's seventh
birthday the following month.

'I don't like ginger,' she said and she wrinkled
her nose, 'but jam and butter icing is always
nice; and cherry.'

'I suppose you'll just have to wait and see,'
laughed Clarissa, 'it couldn't possibly be nicer
than my chocolate one! If only we could thank
her, but she's always fast asleep.'

'She's nocturnal like Mathilde, and Mother,'
said Alexander. 'Maybe it's something to do
with this house.'

They packed the chocolate cake into the picnic basket, with some bread and cheese and lemonade, and walked along to the park. Claudia sat baby Antoine on a blanket on the grass though he was now able to run away if he wanted but if Claudia told him to sit on the blanket he would happily stay there. Then Clarissa spread a green and white checked cloth and they emptied the basket onto it and began to eat.

They had almost forgotten about the hat and the umbrella though Clarissa sometimes woke at night and wondered if it had gone off to terrorise some other person. She also thought about Marvello and how he was so in love with Mother, and of course there was the mysterious accident that had befallen Lisa that no one wanted to talk about.

But today was her birthday and the sun was warm, and they had chocolate cake, and nothing could be nicer!

CHAPTER 12

JUNE

'I WOULD LIKE KIPPERS and buttered toast for breakfast,' declared Alexander one morning.

Clod clapped her hands, 'Oh, I'd forgotten all about the breakfast game! Where are the menus?'

'Well, I know what I fancy,' said Claudia, 'scrambled eggs, please!'

'Mushrooms and tomatoes, with a poached egg,' said Clarissa.

'Bread and jam,' cried Clod.

'But you always have bread and jam, Clod,' said Alexander.

'That's because it's what I like most!' said Clod.

Chloe chose strawberry ice cream even though everyone said it wasn't normally something that people ate for breakfast. Then Claudia went to the kitchen pantry to fetch the bread and jam, and Clarissa went to make the jug of hot chocolate.

Five minutes later they heard screams from the hallway.

'Don't tell me that the hat is back,' gasped Chloe, 'Clarissa will go quite mad.'

The door opened and Claudia and Clarissa came into the dining room. They were each carrying a large tray and both trays were piled high with delicious things to eat, in fact, all the things they had chosen, including Chloe's strawberry ice cream.

'Floss is asleep,' announced Clarissa as she and Claudia handed out the plates, 'so how can she be the one who cooks? And anyway, it would be nearly impossible for anyone to make all this so quickly.'

'And where would anyone get strawberry ice cream?' said Claudia as she spooned scrambled egg onto baby Antoine's dish.

'It's the white gloves,' said Clod, and they all stared at her.

'I'm sure Floss has something to do with it but, and I should have mentioned it before, my hands felt very odd when I put the white gloves on.'

Claudia shook her head, 'Why didn't we realise that something strange was happening?'

'It was because we were just happy to eat it,' said Alexander, 'and I still am!'

This had turned into a very perplexing situation, how could they refuse such delicious food, especially as no one had bothered to cook for them for years? And, after all, there was little point in wasting it so everyone agreed that they would continue as things were.

'No one was coming to any harm,' explained Claudia, 'and even if Floss was somehow involved she was quite able to catch up on her sleep as she did little else.'

However, they did decide that in future they would happily eat bread and jam for breakfast as there was no point in being greedy. Then they went for a long walk in the park.

It was the following day that everything went wrong.

Clarissa went to the front door just after breakfast to check the weather, as someone did every morning. It was very hot, the sun was reflecting off the pavements even though it was still early, and the grass was beginning to turn yellow.

'It's warm out here today,' she called to the others, 'we should go out for a whole day and make the most of the good weather.'

It was a long day and a very enjoyable one but

I won't tell you about it in detail as I'm quite sure you're waiting for the bit where everything went wrong.

And it went just about as wrong as it could possibly go!

CHAPTER 13

POOR OLD FLOSS!

I T WAS ABOUT four in the afternoon when
they returned home feeling hot and tired
after the walk back from the boating lake.
Alexander and Claudia carried the
perambulator up the front steps while Clarissa
and Chloe helped baby Antoine, and Clod
unlocked the front door.

Floss was lying flat on her back next to the
carved trunk, and sitting on her chest was
Mathilde the old cat. She was licking at
something on Floss's nose, it looked like cream.

'It is cream,' said Alexander, when he went to
look. Then he pushed the cat aside and put his
head on her chest to listen for a heartbeat.

'I think she might be dead,' he mumbled,
'though it's hard to tell for sure.'

Claudia picked up baby Antoine and they all
stared down at Floss who looked very peaceful
and just fast asleep.

'She looks much the same as she ever did when she was alive,' stated Chloe in a matter of fact voice, 'but we had better call the Doctor.'

'I just want to check something,' said Clod, and she disappeared into the kitchen. 'I thought as much...' they heard her yell, 'the white gloves have exhausted her completely, and now she's dead!' And she started to wail.

Clarissa and Chloe were first on the scene, quickly followed by Alexander, Claudia, and baby Antoine. Clod was in floods of tears, 'I should have got rid of them along with the hat and the umbrella,' she wailed.

They gazed around in awe. Every surface was covered with cakes, or pies, or some other delicious confection, all beautifully iced, or smothered in cream. There were jars of marmalade and jam, and fruit preserves, and tins full of little sweets, and fairy cakes. One white glove could be seen poking out from beneath the dresser and the other was halfway down the cushioned seat of Floss's old patchwork chair.

Everyone was silent, except for Clod who continued to wail and explain, between choking sobs, that it was all her fault and she really should have realised before poor Floss died of exhaustion.

'We have to tell Mother,' said Clarissa. 'You

do it, Alexander as you're the only boy, apart from baby.'

Alexander reluctantly agreed and they all waited in the kitchen while he went upstairs and tapped gently on her door and called through the keyhole, 'Mother, I have some bad news, I'm afraid.'

After a while a small voice murmured, 'Come in Alexander,' so he went in. The room was very warm and shady and lying on the pink chaise was a woman he barely recognised as his Mother. She looked so pale and fragile even though she had rouge on her cheeks and pale blue shadow on her eyelids.

'I'm afraid Floss has died,' he said.

'Oh, dear, that's too bad,' she murmured softly and that was all.

'We thought you might want to know,' said Alexander, he was puzzled by her silence. 'We've decided to call the doctor because he will know what to do.'

She smiled, 'How very sensible you are Alexander, so like your dear Father.'

Alexander was tempted to ask how she, or anyone for that matter, could possibly know anything about his father, but fortunately before he had the chance she added,

'Will you fetch me my rose water, dear? And my smelling salts.'

Alexander went to her dressing table; it was piled high with boxes of face powder, and bottles of perfume, and pressed posies of flowers that had faded and lost their colour, just like Mother. She took the rose water from him in her frail hands and sprinkled it on her forehead and both white wrists then held the bottle of smelling salts under her nose and lay back on the pink chaise and closed her eyes.

Alexander waited for a few minutes but she didn't stir so he left the room and went back downstairs.

'I'll go for the Doctor,' he said, 'he lives just at the end of the street and I think Mother is too upset to do anything about it so we will have to sort everything out.'

'Of course, as usual!' muttered Clod crossly.

Alexander came back almost straight away with Doctor Gallon who had known them all since they were babies. The Doctor looked very serious when he found Floss lying on the floor in the hall.

He shook his head gravely, 'This won't do; you're all much too young to deal with this. Where are your parents?'

'Mother is overcome with grief,' said Claudia by way of excuse for her absence, 'and she's lying down in her room.'

'Well, this is most irregular,' said the Doctor. 'I'll call an ambulance and the undertaker; and I'll send the bill to your Father. The undertaker will tell you about the funeral.' He shook his head again, 'Get me a sheet please, Claudia, we'll cover her up until they get here, I don't think the cat should be licking her nose.'

He smiled kindly at them, 'You're very sensible children, and you knew exactly what to do. Now I think you should just sit quietly in the library. I will come back and deal with the undertaker so you won't have to.'

They trailed off to the library and sat down quietly on the chewed sofa. Chloe began to plait her hair, and then she said very solemnly,

'We have a whole kitchen full of cakes and pies and it will be impossible for us to eat them all so I propose a cake sale.'

Clarissa was horrified, 'Chloe, really, how can you think of such things when poor Floss is, at this very moment, lying dead in the hall!'

'From exhaustion,' cried Clod, and she started to wail all over again.

'Chloe is right,' said Alexander. 'It would be

71

terrible if it all went to waste and I think a cake sale is an excellent idea! Floss would have wanted us to appreciate them. Of course the Saturday clean up will be out of the question, we can't find the time for both.'

He got up after that and went over to the shelves to find some books to show baby Antoine who especially liked the ones with pictures of Zanzibar and Kathmandu. Claudia was convinced that one day he would be a great explorer but at the moment she had other, more important, things on her mind. 'I think the cake idea is a very good one,' she said at last. 'We need the money in case we decide to visit Mimzi Mai and our friends at the theatre again. None of it is our fault; we didn't invite the hat, or the umbrella and the white gloves, they just turned up of their own accord. Do stop weeping, Clod, nobody blames you. Now, let's plan the cake sale as it will take our minds off what is happening in the hall.'

The hall at that moment was a hive of activity. Doctor Gallon was there along with his colleague who had to sign the death certificate, and there were several people from the undertakers who buzzed around sighing sympathetically as it was their job to do that.

The front door slammed behind them at last; they had all departed, along with Floss.

Only the Doctor remained, he tapped on the door to tell them that it was safe to come out and he mentioned again how clever they were, 'And tell your Mother to call in please, when she feels up to it.'

'Well that will be never,' mumbled Clod.

CHAPTER 14

THE CAKE SALE

T HEY DECIDED THAT Saturday would be the most suitable day for the cake sale and as it was already Friday everything would still be fresh.

The stall, two footstools with a wooden plank across them, could be right by the big iron railings near the main entrance to the park and the boating lake. Lots of people would walk by during the day and it was near enough to replenish the stall from home when they ran out of supplies. Clod searched in vain for the white gloves but they had disappeared so she assumed that Claudia had disposed of them to save her feelings. She was sad that there would be no birthday cake waiting for her but she had come to the conclusion that this would be her punishment for not telling everyone about her suspicions regarding the white gloves.

The cake stall turned out to be far more of a success than they could possibly have imagined. The cakes looked so delicious; there were sponges with butter cream filling, and chocolate cakes, and fruit cakes bursting with sultanas and cherries. As for the pies, no one could believe how mouth watering they were and there was soon a line of people right along the street. Alexander and Chloe went back to the house at regular intervals for replacements but they made sure to keep enough for themselves for a week at least. The pastries wouldn't last that long but the tins of biscuits and jars of preserves could be stored.

Everyone else took turns helping baby Antoine to sail his small boat on the lake so that he didn't get too bored, or fall in, but by mid-afternoon everything was gone and a big pile of coins lay in the bottom of the perambulator.

'Floss would be very pleased that everyone wanted her cakes,' said Clod, 'so maybe I don't feel quite so dreadful about it all.'

'I've never seen this much money in my whole life,' gasped Alexander, 'we can go on as many bus rides as we please now.'

'Wouldn't it be wonderful to go to one of

those little cafes for lemonade,' said Chloe, 'perhaps we might next time we go to visit Mimzi at the theatre?'

Claudia yawned, 'Come on, it's time to go home. I'm really tired and don't forget, there's a cheese flan for supper.'

'I wonder if the white gloves would help me to make such delicious cakes,' said Clarissa. 'Perhaps when we've eaten everything I might put them on and try, though right now I just want to sit down, my feet really hurt.'

'You would have to find the white gloves first though,' said Clod, 'I couldn't find them at all and I thought one of you must have thrown them away.'

But no one could say where they had gone; only that they had mysteriously disappeared from the kitchen but, as we shall see, the white gloves hadn't gone at all. Oh, no! They still had work to do!

CHAPTER 15

DOCTOR GALLON

ON TUESDAY, DOCTOR Gallon came to see them and brought with him a large jug of onion soup and a chicken casserole.

'My wife made these for you,' he said, 'she's concerned that no one is looking after you while your mother is indisposed.'

Claudia thanked him and assured him that they were able to look after themselves as Mama was often unwell. And then she explained that the house was only a little bit dusty as they had been too busy to do the usual Saturday clean.

'Might I go up and visit her?' he asked.

'I'll show you the way,' said Alexander and he led Doctor Gallon through the hall and up the long staircase to Mother's room at the far end of the corridor.

'Good luck,' he whispered, which the Doctor thought a rather strange thing for a son to say and he watched with a bewildered expression as Alexander tiptoed down the stairs.

He came down soon after, 'I'm afraid your Mother is in a state of shock,' he declared in a grave voice. 'Maybe we should find someone to help now that you no longer have Floss. I will see what I can do.'

He patted Clod very gently on the head and smiled at them all. 'The funeral is on Thursday and I've written everything down for you,' and he gave Claudia a card with the time and all the other details such as the hymns and a map of where the church was.

'It will only be us,' said Claudia, 'and we know where the church is, but thank you for arranging it all.'

'We have very loud voices,' added Clod.

'Well, my wife has a very good voice and she will be there, although it would be nice if your Mother is well enough to accompany you. I hope she will be better soon. It must have been a terrible shock for her.'

Clarissa opened the front door and he went off down the steps, 'You're very kind,' she called after him, 'and thank you for the onion soup and the chicken. You can have your pots back on Thursday.'

The house was indeed in need of a clean. There were so many crumbs on the dining room floor that the mice were hard-pressed to eat them before the next shower was dropped from the table. And webs were starting to stretch from one end of the ceiling to the other in a fine veil occupied by spiders of every colour and variety.

The beds were never made, nor the sheets changed, and a thick layer of dust covered every surface.

They put on the dreariest things they could find for the funeral service which wasn't difficult as everything looked dreary and past its best.

Chloe pulled at her old brown skirt that was at least two sizes too small, though the hem had been taken down by Clarissa more than once.

'At least we always had mashed potato when Floss was alive,' she sighed, 'and I wonder who will buy our clothes now that Floss is gone.'

Floss had ordered their clothes by post; parcels that turned up from time to time containing old-fashioned dresses for the girls and trousers for Alexander. They were usually too short or too long and almost always had to be altered. Claudia and Clarissa were old enough to remember being taken on the bus to shop in Paris for new clothes with Mama and Papa, but that was many years ago; life was exciting then.

'I'm sure everything will sort itself out,' said Claudia but she looked doubtful, 'eventually...' she added.

'Things can't get any worse than they are already;' declared Alexander, 'come on, we mustn't be late for Floss.'

The Doctor's wife was waiting for them outside the church and she smiled encouragingly at them in turn. 'My, you do look nice,' she exclaimed quite convincingly, and she straightened Clod's hat and took out a long ribbon to tie back Chloe's curtain of hair; then she said, 'I would be so pleased if you could call me Marie.'

The Vicar looked around expectantly as they walked into the church and sat in the front pew and then he waited for quite a while until Alexander said at last,

'It's only us, you know. She didn't know anyone else apart from Mother,' and he sighed and added as an after-thought, 'and Mathilde, and they couldn't come.'

'Mathilde is her cat,' explained Clod earnestly.

'And Mother...?' The Vicar looked at the

Doctor's wife for explanation and she shook her head gravely, and put her finger to her lips.

'Oh, I see,' said the Vicar, though really he didn't, 'then we will proceed.'

The funeral wasn't long and afterwards Marie insisted that they came back for tea. The Doctor's house was warm and smelled of flowers and was prettily decorated in pinks and creams with pictures on the walls and flowery curtains. It made Clarissa feel sad when she thought of their gloomy, untidy house that was always chilly except for when the kitchen stove was on.

They had boiled eggs and fingers of bread and butter and an apple each. Then Marie told them that once they had three small children but now they had all grown up and loved to visit; the eldest had two tiny daughters called Amelia and Charlotte; and she cooed over baby Antoine and said he was 'an absolute delight!'

The sun was going down as they walked back along the Rue Gladioli. The Doctor's wife was sad to see them go and they promised that they would call again soon.

Clarissa's heart sank when she saw that their front door was wide open.

'I suppose we did leave in a hurry,' she said,

'unless that hat has returned and mysteriously opened the door,' though she whispered this bit because she didn't want to frighten the little ones.

'There's nothing to steal anyway!' said Alexander; and Clod yawned and added 'Well, I don't care, so long as they haven't stolen my bed!'

CHAPTER 16

THE BAKER'S BOY

THE HOUSE FELT strange, even quieter than usual, and there was an unfamiliar smell that they noticed as soon as they walked into the hallway.

Claudia stopped and sniffed, 'Lavender polish!' she exclaimed, 'It smells lovely!'

'I think someone has washed the floor,' said Chloe, 'look, there are little puddles here and there, and the carved trunk and hallstand are all shiny because the dust has gone!'

'No more cobwebs and no more spiders,' announced Clod happily, 'so it's my favourite kind of burglar!'

They stood in the hall for a moment or two longer then Clarissa very cautiously opened the door to the dining room and poked her head around.

'What's happened,' asked Alexander and then, when Clarissa didn't reply, he thrust open the door and they all gazed around in astonishment.

The table gleamed and the floor was swept clean of crumbs, even the spiders' webs that had gradually grown from one side to the other until the ceiling began to look shrouded and misty, were gone.

At the far end of the room something very peculiar was going on; the baker's boy was at the top of a tall ladder and they noticed straight away that he was wearing the white gloves. He was frantically rubbing at a patch of damp on the ceiling with a bright orange duster and he was muttering to himself in a distracted fashion. He hadn't appeared to notice them at all as he was so engrossed in his task.

'Hello,' called Claudia, and she coughed politely to get his attention. It seemed to break the spell because he turned around and gazed at the little huddle in the doorway looking at him with wide eyes and open mouths. He dropped the yellow duster straight away and stared after it with a worried expression then he fell backwards off the ladder and landed on the floor with a bang where he straightaway fell fast asleep.

'Take off the white gloves,' screamed Clod,

'before he goes the same way as Floss!' and she hid her eyes.

Alexander scanned the room appreciatively and gave a low whistle, 'He's done a good job though.'

'Yes, we won't have to clean for weeks!' said Chloe and she laughed and they all joined in and the house rang with laughter for the first time since Floss had departed.

Claudia put a cushion under his head and carefully pulled off the white gloves which were a little too tight.

'He looks very tired,' she whispered, so as not to wake him, then she rolled the gloves into a ball, 'and these can go in the trunk in the hall until we decide what best to do with them.'

After that they went into the kitchen; it was warm and it gleamed for every surface had been scrubbed and polished. Even the fireplace was swept and cleared of ashes, and glowed with bright flames. In the centre of the kitchen table was a vase of flowers and next to the vase, on a china plate, was a large fruit cake.

'I wonder...' said Chloe, and she threw open the larder door. Every shelf was crammed with tarts and pies, and cakes, and flans, and biscuits, 'How is it possible,' she murmured, 'it has to be magic!'

'No wonder the baker's boy is tired,' declared Claudia.

'Well I hope he doesn't die too!' exclaimed Clod. 'It might seem very suspicious if he does, we could all be taken off to prison!'

They ran through the house gasping with astonishment for every room seemed to be tidier and cleaner that the last. The front parlour shone and smelled of flowers, even the old Aspidistra was green and glossy. The beds were made with freshly ironed sheets and the bath had been scrubbed, and the taps shone.

Clarissa sighed, 'It makes me feel tired just looking at it all, and the poor baker's boy will sleep for a week at least. I wonder where he lives, we should take him home.'

'And say what exactly?' asked Alexander. 'I just think it's a pity he never got round to the garden, and the windows could do with a clean. We should have stayed out longer.'

'No, he would have been dead for sure,' said Clod, and she took baby Antoine back to the kitchen for cake even though he had eaten quite a lot already.

'Can I come in?' called a voice from the open front door that no one had bothered to close. 'What a beautiful house you've got here, my, oh my, it's spotless! I don't suppose you've seen my delivery boy, have you? Only I've called at every door on his round, and he's never gone missing before.'

'This way, please,' said Clarissa and she led him down the hall and opened the dining room door. The baker's boy was stretched out flat on his back, just as they had left him, and the room vibrated with his snores.

'I am so sorry!' stammered the baker. 'Whatever can he have been thinking of? He's never done this before; I'll sack him straight away!'

'Oh, please don't,' cried Clarissa.

'No please don't!' cried the others.

The baker looked bewildered and shuffled his feet awkwardly as if he couldn't wait to get away.

'It's not his fault,' said Claudia, 'perhaps he's ill?'

'Yes, he could be ill,' said Clarissa, 'and he's worn out with delivering bread, perhaps?'

They could hardly explain that the baker's boy had been bewitched by a pair of white gloves that had made him clean and polish the house from top to bottom, not to mention the ironing and the baking.

'I'll have to wake him up; he's much too large for me to carry...' he shook his head, 'Well I never, I must have overworked him.'

'Must have,' muttered Alexander,

'Yes, you must have,' agreed Chloe.

But the baker's boy wouldn't wake no matter how much he shook him and shouted his name in his ear.

'I think you should come back for him in the morning,' said Claudia at last.

'But what about his round, I'll never get my bread out, I can't bake and deliver!'

'We'll send him round first thing,' promised Claudia and he departed clicking his tongue and shaking his head in a puzzled fashion. 'I've worked him too hard,' he muttered, 'I'll have to hire another assistant, my profits will go right down!'

'I bet he didn't clean Mother's room though,' said Alexander when he had gone, 'she wouldn't have liked that at all!'

Then they had supper and went to bed.

The baker's boy was still snoring when they got up the next morning, and he was still stretched out flat on his back in exactly the same position with his mouth open.

'At least he isn't catching spiders; he would

have swallowed dozens last week!' said Alexander and he gave him a shake.

He stirred and muttered 'Where am I?' Then he turned onto his side and went back to sleep without even waiting for a reply.

'I'll get a blanket for him,' said Clarissa, 'the floor must be so cold and we should eat in the kitchen, there's no reason to disturb him.'

They sat at the shiny breakfast table eating yesterday's bread because there had been no delivery owing to the baker's boy being fast asleep in the dining room. Their lives had changed but, to be honest, not greatly. Father would still pay the bills, and Mother would mope all day on her pink chaise. Even Floss wouldn't be missed that much as she did so little, and they still had Mathilde who at that very moment was rubbing against their legs and purring softly.

'I'm bored,' moaned Clod, 'and I want a Mother; and perhaps even a real Father who would care about us and look after us. It's almost like being an orphan, especially now that Floss has gone too.'

Mathilde mewed softly at the mention of Floss so Chloe picked her up.

'Poor Mathilde, you still have us, and the mice will soon be back.'

She opened the door to the kitchen garden and put her down in the vegetable patch. 'We could clear up the garden ourselves; it would give us something interesting to do.'

'We could even go to school,' suggested Clarissa, 'that's normally what happens, isn't it? Though I think it might be the summer holidays.'

'That's lucky!' said Alexander. And then he and Clod exclaimed both at the same moment, 'School sounds too much like hard work!' so Claudia decided not to mention that the school holidays wouldn't be for a while yet in any case. Instead she filled a basin with water and they left Clod and baby Antoine to play with Mathilde in the vegetable patch while they wandered down into the rambling back garden that was overgrown with roses and lush grass.

'Look,' cried Chloe, 'there's a swing! We don't even need to walk to the park; we can have picnics out here! I'd forgotten all about the garden!'

They didn't see their Mother's pale face as she watched them from her window; or her sad smile as they chased each other through the trees.

The baker's boy had gone when they went

back into the house and the only sign that he had been there at all was the cushion and the blanket on the floor, an upturned ladder, several yellow dusters and mops, and, of course, the fact that everything gleamed as if a whole army of housemaids had been around to clean.

CHAPTER 17

THE 14ᵀᴴ JULY!

TIME PASSED AND the remarkable incident
with the baker's boy was almost forgotten,
which meant that the dust was back as they had
been so busy making the garden beautiful. They
cut the grass, and pulled out weeds and
trimmed the roses. On fine evenings they lit
candles and stood them along the pathways so
it looked all green and mysterious. They also
became quite used to cooking their own meals
as the grocery van came and delivered their
usual order just as if Floss were still alive.
Sometimes they left little notes like, 'please
leave sausages' and they cooked them over a
fire in the garden as the light grew dim, and
owls swooped, and giant moths flapped
through the trees.

The house and garden had begun to feel
almost magical. No one mentioned the hat, or
the umbrella, or even the little white gloves that

were snuggled in the trunk in the hallway getting up to all kinds of mischief.

Now and then, Marie, the Doctor's wife, came by with luxuries like the onion soup and she always told them how clever and grown-up they had become; and how wonderful the garden looked. Mother remained the same but occasionally her pale face would appear at the window of her bedroom though no one ever seemed to notice.

Clod's seventh birthday had been and gone; they celebrated with a sponge cake made by Claudia and Alexander, and decorated by Clarissa and Chloe in pink and white frosting. They never thought to unleash the power of the white gloves but anyone watching the transformation taking place in their lives might have suspected that some of the magic was still leaking out of the old carved trunk, though now the magic was good. There were no more scrabbling colonies of rabbits with bristling whiskers and pink noses, just waiting for someone to lift the lid; and Clarissa's dreams were all sweet ones.

It was the tenth of July, a few days before Claudia's birthday on the fourteenth which is a day of celebration throughout France. The day was hot and they were sunning themselves on a patch of grass under the apple tree while Clod made daisy chains with baby Antoine.

'Why don't we spend some of our money from the cake sale? We could go into the city for the parade,' suggested Clarissa. 'How odd that we never thought to spend it before; I suppose it was because we didn't have anything to spend it on but it would be nice to visit Mimzi.'

'Good idea, and maybe walk up to Montmartre to see if Pierre is about,' added Chloe, as she treasured her portrait and had propped it up in front of an ancient photograph of Great Aunt Hortense in the front parlour.

'And I still want to find out what happened to Lisa, the magician's glamorous assistant,' continued Clarissa; and then, 'I don't know why I said that,' because the others were staring at her in horror as if a spell had been broken.

'And I wish I hadn't as it's made me think of the horrible hat, and the elegant umbrella, and I had quite forgotten about them.'

Baby Antoine came to sit on Claudia's lap, 'Mimzi,' he cried, 'I like Mimzi.' He had become quite good at talking as he was no longer a little baby.

'It's an excellent idea,' said Claudia, 'and we don't have to go to the theatre although it would be nice to see Mimzi Mai and Hirondelle and the others.'

'They've probably forgotten who we are anyway,' sighed Clod and she flicked at a bee that landed on her leg.

'Of course they haven't forgotten us!' said Alexander indignantly.

They got up very early to go into Paris as they knew the buses would be crowded and everywhere would be bustling with people; also because it was Claudia's birthday and she was going to be fourteen, which was very exciting. She secretly hoped that Mother might suddenly remember and come down to breakfast but she wasn't surprised when she didn't, it would have been too much to hope for. Everyone sang 'Happy Birthday' and then they went out onto the sunny street to catch the bus into the city.

All along the Rue Gladioli there were blue, white and red flags draped from windows and balconies. They billowed in the breeze and flapped noisily from poles above the railings of the park. It was a sea of colour as men in top hats and ladies in their Sunday best pushed their way along the pavement to the bus stop.

Crowds of children in bright clothes and sun hats accompanied them, all waving tiny flags or carrying posies of flowers. Some went into the park; people with overladen picnic baskets, mothers with giggling babies on their hips, or little ones who were holding toy boats and balloons, and fathers hoisting toddlers onto their shoulders.

It wasn't long before the bus came and they scrambled on board. It was already crowded but they managed to find seats in the second row from the front behind some noisy children who shrieked and bounced with excitement.

'None of this would have happened if it wasn't for the hat!' exclaimed Clarissa suddenly as they gazed through the windows at the crowds.

'I never thought I would say that but now it has gone for good maybe I can see that it has made our lives more interesting than before. We would never have come into the city on our own before the hat arrived on the doorstep, or had the cake sale.'

'But Floss might still be alive,' murmured Clod sadly.

'Never mind, we still have Mathilde,' said Claudia hoping to comfort her, 'and I'm quite sure that Floss would be happy at how things have worked out.' Then she turned back to baby Antoine and began to point out all the interesting people and things in the street below.

Chloe flicked her long golden hair behind her ears because it was getting in her eyes and needed a ribbon. 'Well I think the nicest thing of all has been visiting Mother's theatre where she sang and had such a lovely time, and meeting Mimzi Mai and Hirondelle and the others. And having my portrait done,' she added as an afterthought.

'Mimzi, Mimzi,' chanted baby Antoine and he clapped his hands.

'And the food, and your birthday cake, Clarissa,' cried Clod,' and the surprise Christmas cake, though I still wonder why Father Christmas doesn't come to our house.'

Claudia smiled, 'Well perhaps he remembered after all and that's where that cake came from.'

'I wonder if the baker's boy has recovered from his enormous spring clean,' said Clarissa, 'though even that turned out quite well because the baker had to take on another boy to help as he was convinced it was all his fault And we had a really clean house, for a while anyway.'

'Well I want to know what happened to Lisa,' declared Alexander suddenly, 'and what did Marvello do that was so dreadful?'

Claudia put her arm around him, 'I'm not sure we'll ever know that, dear, and it's all in the past. Only Hirondelle remembers and she refuses to talk about it. Maybe it upsets her too much.'

'Archie knows!' said Alexander defiantly, then he frowned and added, 'and the hat knows too!'

CHAPTER 18

PARIS

P ARIS WAS A swirling rainbow of colour in
the bright sunshine. It seemed to shimmer
in front of the grey buildings and the green of
the trees, and a clamour of voices rose from the
streets and merged with the chattering voices
on the top deck of the bus.

'We'll get off here,' decided Claudia as the bus
came to a halt and people rose from their seats.
'Come on; stay together or we'll lose each other,
hold hands!'

She picked up baby Antoine and they
climbed down into the crowded streets that
were lined with jostling people waiting for the
parade. They made way reluctantly for the
children as they wound their way through to
the front. Clod clung to Clarissa's skirt so that
she didn't get lost. The sound of music and
marching feet reached them before the soldiers
appeared. They came from all the French

territories including the Foreign Legion with their sand coloured uniforms and strange hats with little flaps that came down over their necks to protect them from the heat of the desert.

They marched past in step, one regiment after another, and their singing seemed to fill the air and the spaces between the grey buildings as the crowds cheered and waved flags; then suddenly it was over and the pavements began to clear.

'There's Mimzi,' yelled Alexander, he pointed and waved, 'and Hirondelle, look, over there.'

Mimzi waved back, 'How lovely to see you all,' she called. She was wearing a blue dress and a straw hat with red and white ribbons, and Hirondelle was in white with a blue hat. It had a wide brim that shielded her face from the sun and was adorned with a sprig of flowers and an artificial bluebird. She and Hirondelle linked arms and pushed their way through the throng towards the children.

'You look so pretty,' gasped Chloe, 'I love your hats!'

Hirondelle smiled, 'How wonderful to see you! I hope you'll come back to the theatre with us, there's a special show this evening and I'm sure we'll fit you in.'

'We're on our way now,' said Mimzi, she bent down and scooped baby Antoine into her arms and kissed him, 'everywhere is very crowded and we have lots of food there. It will be quieter and good to get out of the sun for a while, and it's not too far to walk, please come.'

'We were coming to visit you!' cried Clod.

'Yes, it's one of the reasons we're here!' added Alexander and they set off along the leafy boulevards.

The theatre felt cool and shady after the heat of the sun. Hirondelle and Mimzi took off their hats and put them on a stand in the foyer. 'Let's see who else is here' said Mimzi, 'we can have a feast; it will be fun.'

Albert, the House Manager, was already there, and Salaam the Magician, and Coco, the bendy acrobat. They greeted the children with smiles and hugs and Coco did somersaults and cartwheels all the way up the aisle and across the stage just to show how pleased he was. Alexander looked around for Gerard the Ventriloquist and his puppet Archie but they were nowhere to be seen. He had a few questions he wanted to ask Archie concerning Marvello and the accident that had befallen Lisa, his glamorous assistant.

Then Albert and Salaam closed the heavy curtains and carried an ornate table onto the stage so that it looked like a large gloomy room until someone switched on the lights and the backdrop and scenery were illuminated. The stage was set for the show that evening which was to be a celebration of France past and present. It was hung about with flags and the backdrop was painted to represent a Parisian street but the centre part was supposed to look like the inside of a palace. It had painted-on chairs of gold, and large mirrors, and rich tapestries. It was very beautiful and everyone agreed that it looked almost real.

The sound of laughter came from the foyer then the door to the auditorium flew open and Louisa and Francesca came bustling in with a flurry of petticoats.

'It's so hot outside,' complained Francesca and she sank into the nearest seat, fanning her face with one hand. Louisa ran down the aisle towards them, 'Look, Francesca, the beautiful children are back, and the chubby baby!' and she rushed up the steps onto the stage through a gap in the curtains and hugged them in turn.

'Oh, the chubby baby,' cried Francesca, and she leapt out of her seat and followed Louisa.

CHAPTER 19

THE MYSTERIOUS ACCIDENT

THEY HAD A lovely time and the food was scrumptious but I'm sure that you are as anxious as Alexander to get to the part where he asks Archie what happened to Lisa, Marvello's assistant. And whether the tragic accident had anything to do with the way Mother was now; not to mention the sinister hat!

But first, the show!

The theatre filled very quickly that evening. No one wanted the day to end, and it was cool and restful and somewhere to sit after a long afternoon in the sunshine.

People poured in, their faces pink and glowing from the heat, all undoing their top buttons and exchanging greetings and gossip. Claudia sat with baby Antoine on her knee, and Clod and Chloe shared a seat. Only Clarissa and Alexander had seats of their own but it meant they only took up four places instead of six.

Soon the auditorium was completely full and Albert had to turn people away before closing the doors. Everyone gazed at the closed curtains in anticipation as the lights dimmed, the chatter ceased, and silence fell. A bright light fell over their rapt faces when the curtains parted and the music began. Albert was centre stage in a long powdered wig of the type worn by King Louis the sixteenth, and Hirondelle was dressed as Marie Antoinette his Queen. They did a sketch about the French revolution and then a cardboard guillotine was hauled on stage and the theatre erupted with laughter when Coco came on dressed as a revolutionary and chased them up and down the aisles and into the audience.

Most popular of all was Gerard the Ventriloquist, though really we should say Archie because he was the one who did all the talking. He sat on Gerard's knees and scanned the audience with his shiny dark eyes until they came to rest on the six children in the front row.

'Strange things happen in Paris still,' he declared in his odd unearthly voice, and his eyelids opened and shut twice; then he turned his head stiffly to look directly at Alexander and his left eye closed and snapped open again with a loud click.

'He winked at me!' whispered Alexander, and he shuddered and sank down further into his seat, but Archie wasn't finished.

'Did you hear about the magician who sawed a lady in half?'

'It's only a trick, fake, just like you,' called a man from the audience.

'Yes, you'll be telling us next that white rabbits appear out of thin air,' shouted a second man and everyone laughed and applauded.

'White rabbits do appear out of thin air,' whispered Clarissa, 'we've seen them.'

'You mean you don't believe in magic,' said Archie, 'but magic is all around us!' And his glass eyes rolled and came back to settle on Alexander. Then he guffawed in a menacing way and turned his head towards Gerard in a jerky fashion so that it seemed for a moment as if it would roll off. 'Did you hear that? They don't believe in magic but we do, don't we? Go on, tell them, Gerard; tell them about the lady that was sawn in half.'

Gerard spoke then, 'Oh, Archie, don't frighten the audience, it's just a joke ladies and gentlemen and a wonderful trick as you will see later in the show; but don't let on to Salaam that I've told you his secret.'

And he put his hand firmly around Archie's mouth while the puppet squirmed to get free. The audience thought it was all part of the show and they laughed and clapped when Gerard leapt to his feet and dragged the kicking Archie into the wings.

Albert was waiting for him, 'That's it,' he hissed, 'get out, and don't come back until you have a dummy that knows how to behave! Quick, Louisa, Francesca, the dance routine, now!'

But Albert need not have worried. Everyone in the audience was in high spirits and when Salaam came on stage with Mimzi and told them that he was going to saw her in half they all applauded and cheered. It went silent when Mimzi climbed into a long wooden box and he closed the lid. Salaam began to saw and when he had finished he parted the two halves of the box just to show that he really had sawn her in half. There was a collective gasp from the audience as they remembered Archie's words but they had no need to fear. After a few moments Salaam waved his wand in a shower of golden sparks and pushed the two halves back together and opened the lid. Mimzi climbed out; she was back in one piece and she curtsied and Salaam bowed and everyone stood up and cheered.

'How did he do that?' asked Clod, 'It must be magic!'

'It's just the way the box is made,' said Alexander quietly, 'I've read about it. There's a space for Mimzi to hide her legs so that she's only in one half of the box and is never really cut in two. Unless something goes horribly wrong,' he added.

Coco came on next; he was an amazing juggler as well as an acrobat but his grand finale was a fire eating act. The audience was transfixed but Alexander couldn't concentrate at all.

'Clarissa, I have to find Gerard,' he whispered, 'I'll see you afterwards.'

'Come back, Alexander,' she murmured as he crept past her and made for the nearest door at the side of the stage.

A dark narrow staircase led to the dressing rooms, Gerard would be there, he was certain of that, and Archie. Alexander knocked on the door but there was no reply though he could hear the sound of someone sobbing so he turned the handle and went in. Gerard was sitting in front of a large mirror and his face was streaked with tears that made white furrows through his thick stage makeup.

He looked up at Alexander 'This is your fault,' he said, and tears began to pour down his cheeks again. 'If it wasn't for your Mother none of this would have happened. Marvello would never have sawn Lisa in half,' and he buried his face in his hands. 'Forget I said that; it was an accident, just an accident.'

'Oh no it wasn't, it wasn't an accident at all!' Alexander turned around; Archie was sitting in the corner propped against a chair leg and his glass eyes were peering around the room.

Gerard glared at Archie as the sound of applause and loud cheers echoed up from the auditorium. 'Albert told me to leave the theatre; he said I can't return unless I find a new dummy. The show has finished and now I must leave before Albert comes backstage.'

Archie swivelled his head until he was looking straight at Alexander, 'I saw it all, and I heard what Marvello said to Serafina afterwards.'

'Stop,' cried Gerard, 'you're only supposed to speak through me!' He leapt from his seat and went to seize the dummy but Archie seemed to come to life and dodged to one side. 'I know what happened because I was in the room when he told Serafina that he meant to saw Lisa in half because he wanted to be free to marry her!'

'Stop!' cried Gerard again and he leapt forward and grabbed him by the throat. 'We've heard enough!' He opened a large suitcase and thrust the kicking and protesting Archie inside.

'It was the Chinese magician that let me speak so that I could tell you what really happened to Lisa,' he screamed, as Gerard slammed the lid and locked it.

'Are you still here?' asked Albert angrily as he came through the door, 'I told you to go. Find another dummy; you should throw that one into the river. Do you hear me, Gerard, go, now! Alexander, your sisters and little brother are waiting for you downstairs.'

'I'm really sorry,' gasped Alexander, 'I just needed to find out!'

'I know, and it isn't your fault so go now and we'll speak later.'

Albert stood to one side and Gerard pushed past carrying the suitcase containing Archie. They could still hear him kicking and protesting as Gerard rushed down the stairs, and when the side door to the theatre opened they felt a blast of cool evening air before it slammed shut again, and the Ventriloquist was gone.

Alexander ran down then and back into the auditorium where the others were waiting. Everyone else had left, apart from the cast members who were on stage staring down at them with expressions of concern on their faces. Claudia looked worried, 'Where have you been, Alexander? You should have stayed with us.'

'And you missed the fire eating,' said Clod, 'Coco is amazing!'

'Gerard has gone, for good,' said Albert. 'We mustn't let any of this ruin such a wonderful day. I know everyone is tired so I think we should sweep the stage and depart. There will be plenty of time to talk tomorrow.'

CHAPTER 20

ZEN XIANG
AND LIN XU

AFTERWARDS, WHEN THEY were snuggled up in Mimzi's cosy little apartment it all seemed impossible. How could a ventriloquist's dummy come to life? Soon Clod and baby Antoine were fast asleep, no doubt dreaming of jugglers and magicians, and the night was quiet and cool; even the noises of revellers in the streets had faded.

Someone was tapping on the door and Mimzi hurried to open it. It was Hirondelle. She smiled at them all and found a place to sit next to Chloe on the rug.

'I think it's time someone told you the whole story,' she said. 'It isn't fair for you to wonder, and everything is worse when you only have half a story, isn't that right, Chloe?' and she gave her a squeeze.

'Apart from Gerard, and Archie, I am the only

one who was part of the troop when it happened. I'm afraid it's true; Lisa was sawn in half by Marvello! You mustn't worry too much though,' she added when she saw their alarmed faces, 'Marvello was also an amazing hypnotist and Lisa didn't feel a thing, not a thing!'

Chloe wrinkled her nose, 'I don't see how it's possible to be sawn in two and not feel a thing. I'm sure I would, even if I was hypnotised, whatever that is.'

'A hypnotist can put you to sleep in such a way that you will obey anything he suggests,' explained Mimzi, 'it's like being under a spell. But please go on, Hirondelle, no one has ever told me the whole story.'

'Everyone knew how much Marvello wanted Serafina but we never thought he would go to such extreme lengths to make her his own, and naturally, Serafina didn't want him. Apart from the fact that he was already married to Lisa he was a strange man, unattractive and sly. None of us could work out why Lisa had married him in the first place.'

'But what happened next,' asked Clarissa, 'after he had sawn her in two?'

'At first we didn't realise anything was amiss. Marvello had performed the trick hundreds of times. On this particular evening Lisa came on stage and curtsied prettily to the audience. She seemed miles away and when I spoke to her, just before she went on, she didn't answer, just looked straight through me as if I wasn't there at all. Then Marvello opened the lid of the box and she climbed in.'

'Don't stop,' murmured Clarissa, 'what happened next?'

'Marvello began to saw through the box then he suddenly threw his arms in the air and gave a terrifying howl before dashing into the wings. We stared at him in astonishment. I think we all wondered if it was part of the act. I'm sure the audience did, to begin with at least, but Marvello rushed straight to his dressing room and we could hear him wailing and moaning how it was an accident, just an accident.' Hirondelle smiled round at their shocked faces, 'I'm sure she didn't know anything about it, dears. Anyway then someone in the audience jumped up and shouted, 'The Magician has cut the lady in half!' and he picked up his two little children and fled out of the theatre. This started a panic, as you can imagine; suddenly everyone was rushing for the door and they were shouting and crying, and carrying on as if the sky was falling in.'

'You can't blame them,' said Claudia, 'it's not the sort of thing that happens every day, is it?'

'Why wasn't Marvello put in prison?' asked Alexander.

'He insisted it was a terrible accident and when someone eventually plucked up enough courage to open the box, Lisa was just lying there, all serene, as if she was having a lovely dream. Marvello said that she must have forgotten to put her legs in the secret compartment.'

'Did you believe him?' asked Chloe.

'Yes, of course,' said Hirondelle, 'we couldn't imagine anyone really sawing a lady in half, not even Marvello. We all believed him, everyone except the Chinese acrobat; his name was Lin Xu and he had fallen in love with Lisa. He didn't believe it at all and he was heartbroken, poor thing!'

'It might have been easier if Marvello had just given Lisa to Lin Xu,' remarked Alexander, 'it would have saved no end of trouble!'

'If only life were that simple,' laughed Mimzi.

'Yes, indeed, except Marvello didn't want anyone else to have Lisa either,' continued Hirondelle, 'and Serafina would never have married Marvello in any case. Lin Xu vowed he would get even with Marvello. He said his father was a great magician, the best magician in China, and probably in the entire world. He once worked for the Emperor who said he was his most valued servant, and more than that, a dear friend, and he showered him with wonderful gifts because he knew that the Maharajah of India wanted him and so too did the Tzar of Russia.

Marvello was terrified because Zen Xiang was renowned throughout the Kingdom of Magicians, and the Magic Circle. I suspect he knew then that he had gone too far and that he would be forever pursued by Zen Xiang. He disappeared soon after and we all thought that it was because he couldn't forgive himself for what had happened.'

'But what happened to Lin Xu?' asked Claudia.

'Poor Lin Xu,' said Hirondelle, 'he ran off into the night and we never saw him again either.'

'It's getting late,' whispered Mimzi. The candle light glimmered in her eyes making them shine and reflecting the room, 'you should sleep now.'

'Just tell me about Archie,' said Alexander quietly, 'what has he got to do with all of this?'

'It's just that Archie was the only one in the room when Marvello admitted to Serafina that it hadn't been an accident at all. He said he had done it just for her. He didn't know that a more powerful magician was already at work and he had given Archie the ability to speak without Gerard and, as you know, a dummy doesn't usually speak unless he is sitting on the knee of a ventriloquist. Archie has been quiet for many years but now he wants you to know what happened, can you think of any reason for that?'

Clarissa and Alexander exchanged glances, 'It could be something to do with the way Mother is now,' said Clarissa, and they told Hirondelle and Mimzi about how sad and remote Mother had become over the years.

They listened intently but then Mimzi insisted they all settle down as it was gone midnight and they had to catch a bus in the morning.
When they woke up Hirondelle and Mimzi had gone. Mimzi had written a note, it said:

Dearest Claudia, Clarissa, Alexander, Chloe, Clodhilde and baby Antoine.

  We have to go to the theatre to get everything ready for the show tonight; you were all fast asleep when we left and we didn't want to

116

*wake you. Yesterday was such an eventful day
and we know how tired you were.*

*Thank you so much for coming to see us and
we hope you weren't too frightened by Archie,
or by what happened to poor Lisa. Come back
and see us soon.*

Please slam the door when you leave.

*With Much Love and affection,
Mimzi and Hirondelle xx*

They sat on the bus in silence, baby Antoine
was still drowsy and before long he was sound
asleep. The others dozed as it jogged along
leaving the city behind.

Eventually Clarissa sighed and turned to
Alexander, 'I'm quite sure that the horrible hat
has something to do with Marvello.'

Claudia was sitting on the other side of the
bus but she overheard, 'I'm certain you are
right, Clarissa,' she said, 'and the elegant
umbrella too.'

'Yes, and the umbrella,' agreed Clarissa, 'but
I'm not sure how. Do you remember the
inscription? It said 'To a valued friend with
grateful thanks', and the handle was made of
gold and probably very valuable.'

'I think it's the Magician's umbrella, a present from the Emperor of China,' declared Alexander, 'not Marvello, the other one, what was he called? Hirondelle said he was the most powerful Magician in the entire world?'

'Zen Xiang was his name. And it was his son, Lin Xu, who said that Zen Xiang would make sure that Marvello was punished for sawing Lisa in two,' said Clarissa, who had a very good memory for names. 'It's very lucky we managed to get rid of the hat and the umbrella when we did! Who knows what would have happened next, they must have arrived on our doorstep for a reason.'

'Perhaps the hat was looking for Mother?' suggested Chloe.

'And maybe the umbrella was watching the hat,' said Clarissa, 'so it's fortunate that we found a way to dispose of them when we did, though it wasn't easy, not easy at all.'

Soon the boating lake appeared in the distance. Some of the flags still remained in the Rue Gladioli and along the park railings and they flapped and billowed as the wind was getting up. It blew the trees and fluttered leaves past the windows and twigs onto the roof of the bus. Claudia picked up baby Antoine as he was still fast asleep and they got off the bus and crossed the road. The pretty copper gate was open and leaves had started to pile up in front of the steps.

Clarissa saw it first, a long parcel done up with brown paper and string. It was wide at one end and narrow at the other and it had a large label stuck on the top. Her heart sank for she had a good idea what was inside as soon as she laid eyes upon it.

'Unclaimed lost property,' she read out loud, 'They're back!' she screamed and gave the box a hefty kick that sent it flying down the steps into the pile of leaves.

No one knew quite what to say; they stood looking down on the box in complete silence until a leaf landed on baby Antoine's nose and he sneezed and woke up struggling to be put down. Clod unlocked the front door and they trooped in. The house felt cold and unwelcoming. The spiders' webs and dust were back and there was no sign of the old cat Mathilde.

Clarissa stood in the doorway, thought a moment then turned around and went back through the front door and down the steps.

'Where is Clarissa going?' asked Chloe, but no one answered.

Clarissa stopped at the bottom and picked up the long brown parcel then she marched back up the steps and through the front door and down the hall to the library where she put it down on the floor while she undid the glass doors to the garden.

'Where are you going, Clarissa?' called Claudia from the hall but she seemed to be in a dream as she stepped out into the garden and set off down the path.

'Do you think she's alright?' asked Chloe.

'It looks to me as if she's decided to leave the parcel at the bottom of the garden,' said Alexander. 'I just hope there's nothing in it that we want to keep.'

'No, it's definitely the horrible hat,' said Claudia.

'And the elegant umbrella,' added Clod.

'We didn't even give our names when we left them at the Lost Property Office,' said Chloe.

'But the hat knows where we live,' said Alexander.

CHAPTER 21

MOTHER

C LARISSA WALKED AS far from the house as she
could. The wind blew her hair back from her
face and she felt a few spots of rain on her cheeks.
Soon she couldn't see the house at all, just trees
and shrubs and clumps of foliage. She couldn't
remember the garden being quite this big. She
seemed to be going down a long slope that
definitely hadn't been there before, then up the
other side and past a stone statue of Neptune. No,
this was the wrong garden but how could that be?

It was time to turn back, she stopped and spun
around, glancing in all directions as the rain
started to pour, drenching her clothes and running
down her face. Which way is home she wondered
as the leaves swirled around her making her feel
dizzy and confused.

'Clarissa...' called a voice, 'it's this way...'

Clarissa dropped the parcel and turned towards
the voice.

It called again, 'Clarissa…' It was a gentle, soothing voice and somehow familiar.

'Mama…?' cried Clarissa and in her mind she could see her Mother's face, pale but smiling, and her fingers beckoning.

'Mama…' cried Clarissa again and she started to run, down the steep slope of the strange garden, past the statue of Neptune, and up the other side. She could see a glimmer of light in the distance and then she was out of the trees and back on the path that led to the house. The rain was lashing against the long windows of the library as she reached them gasping for breath and soaked from head to foot.

Clod opened the door, 'Where have you been?' she asked, 'You're very wet!'

'Yes, we were about to send out a search party,' said Alexander, 'but the garden isn't big enough!'

No one mentioned the parcel so Clarissa sat down on the chewed sofa between Claudia and Chloe, and Clod and Alexander went to join baby Antoine on the moth-eaten rug, and they all went to sleep.

CHAPTER 22

THE DRAGON AND MARVELLO

IT WAS LATE afternoon when Clarissa opened one eye and saw the sun streaming down making gold patterns in the puddles on the path and turning the trees into a beautiful bronze. Then she saw the hat staring in at her from the other side of the glass. She put one hand over her eyes so that she wouldn't have to look at it and shook Claudia's arm with the other until she woke with a start.

'The hat is back,' she whispered.

Claudia leapt off the sofa with a terrifying shriek that woke everyone and made baby Antoine cry.

'How did that happen?' asked Claudia.

Clarissa was in floods of salty tears, they ran down her face and into her mouth.

'I don't know,' she wept, 'I took them as far

into the garden as I possibly could, and I got lost, and Mother called me back.'

'Poor Clarissa,' murmured Chloe, 'I think this is all getting too much for you. It's quite impossible to get lost in our garden.'

'It's too much for all of us,' said Claudia, 'there must be something we can do.'

'I've been asleep for most of the day,' complained Alexander 'and I should like to know why as that has never happened before. Maybe we've been hypnotised, like Lisa, and we're all under the spell of the hat?'

'I don't want to be sawn in half,' cried Clod, and her eyes grew round and she went to hide behind the sofa.

Tap, tap, tap, went the hat against the glass.

'It wants to be let in,' said Alexander, 'I think it's looking for Mother.'

He went over to the window and tapped back, 'Go away!' he cried, 'We don't want you, and neither does Serafina!'

At the mention of her name the hat became very angry; it jumped up and down making strange muttering sounds and throwing itself against the glass of the door. It was Alexander who noticed the umbrella hopping up from behind. It lifted itself into the air and then came down, hitting the hat squarely and sending it flying onto the gravel path.

'Ow...!' yelled a voice from the hat and it tried to get away from the umbrella that was about to deal it another hefty blow.

Then a curious thing happened, the elegant spikes of the umbrella began to change into scalloped wings that were a silky black with indigo tips, and they lifted gracefully with the breeze as the hat struggled to escape.

'No...!' it screamed, 'leave me alone...!'

But a very strange transformation was taking place because the hat had grown long shadowy legs, and a head, and shoulders, and arms.

'Look at the hat,' cried Alexander, 'do you think it's Marvello? And the umbrella, it's changing into a... dragon!'

The shadowy figure started to run down the path and as he ran he slowly became more solid until he resembled a man with long black trousers and a top hat and a short black cape. As for the elegant umbrella, it was vast now, with flapping wings and a golden head where the handle had been. It swooped after Marvello and caught him in one claw and threw him onto his back into the space between his wings, and then he flew off high into the sky.

'It's Zen Xiang's dragon,' whispered Clod admiringly.

'The hat has gone!' cried Clarissa, and she turned away from the window and leapt onto the sofa and bounced up and down joyfully until the stuffing came out and flew around the room like feathery flakes of snow.

CHAPTER 23

THE CARVED TRUNK

I T WAS MUCH later in the evening when they heard strange scrabbling noises coming from the carved trunk in the hall.

Baby Antoine smiled, 'Wabbits,' he murmured, 'I love wabbits.'

'Well I hope it isn't wabbits,' said Clarissa, 'because I've had quite enough of magic and I was hoping it had gone completely. I never thought I would say this but with any luck it's just mice. You open it, Claudia.'

'Must I?' asked Claudia, 'can't someone else do it?'

'Something is happening!' cried Chloe as the carved trunk started to shake violently and the lid was thrust open from inside.

They gasped in surprise when a handsome young man climbed out, he turned to smile at them then he reached into the box and offered his hand to a pretty girl and she climbed out too.

She looked about seventeen and she had long golden curls and was wearing a satin dress of deep rose pink, and, on each hand she wore a little white glove.

'It's Lin Xu, and Lisa,' murmured Clarissa and she clapped her hands.

'So romantic,' sighed Chloe.

Lisa turned and smiled too and they noticed that she had a little gap around her waist where the lower half of her body didn't quite join up with the top. They went through the front door and down the steps and by the time they reached the gate the gap had completely gone and Lisa was all in one piece again. Then they ran off laughing down the street that was all golden in the setting sun.

'Where did they come from?' asked Clod, and she ran to the carved trunk and peered inside.

'Please don't!' cried Claudia, 'if you fall in you might disappear and we'll never see you again!'

'I'm looking for the secret compartment, like the one in the magician's box,' she called back and her voice was muffled because she was leaning in and scrabbling around amongst the gloves and boots on the bottom.

'There won't be anything there now,' said Clarissa, 'it was magic, and I think that's probably the last of it.'

'How can someone who has been sawn in two come back to life?' asked Alexander, and he went to join Clod who had climbed into the carved trunk just to make absolutely certain there was no hidden compartment.

Clarissa looked thoughtful for a moment and then she said, 'For that matter you could just as well ask how it is that a magician can turn into a hat?'

'And how an even more powerful magician could send a dragon in the shape of an umbrella just to make sure that the hat behaves,' added Chloe.

'But why?' asked Clarissa, 'Why did any of it happen at all?'

'It must have been something to do with Marvello looking for Mother,' said Chloe, 'and he couldn't have her so he decided to ruin her life.'

'Well, I suppose he has anyway,' declared Alexander as he climbed out of the trunk, 'and you're right there's nothing there at all and we're back where we started.'

Clod stood up in the trunk, she looked hot

and flustered. 'You don't think Floss is in here too, do you?' she asked, and she gazed down at her feet just to make sure.

'No,' said Claudia, 'sadly I don't but Floss was very old and she had a lovely life with us.'

'I still miss her though,' said Clod, 'she was the nearest thing we had to a mother.'

Alexander sighed, 'And the white gloves, I think I miss those even more!'

CHAPTER 24

THE MAGIC BOX

S O, THERE WE are, all wrapped up neatly, no more mysterious hats, or elegant umbrellas; and certainly no more useful white gloves. They were just six children living in a large house on the outskirts of Paris with an old cat and a melancholy mother who never left her room. The magic had gone from the house but the influence of the evil Marvello remained, though maybe even that would soon be gone, Zen Xiang, the Greatest Magician in the entire world would make sure of it!

It was only a few days later that Clarissa went to the front door to check the weather and there, at the bottom of the steps, was a box that glowed and flared almost as if it were on fire. She shut the door quickly and went back indoors.

'That was quick, has something happened?' called Claudia from the dining room.

'I can't bear it!' said Clarissa sadly, 'I thought everything was back to normal again, well as normal as ever it was. The hat has gone, for good I hope, and the umbrella, and the white gloves, but now we have a box instead!'

'What kind of a box?' asked Claudia, and she went to open the door but Clarissa stood firmly in front of it and barred her way so she tried to look over her shoulder and through the coloured glass instead.

'It's about the size of a small suitcase,' said Clarissa, 'and it's at the bottom of the steps, and if we pretend it isn't there it might just disappear. I think it's a magic box as it has a peculiar glow but I really hope not because I've had quite enough of magic! '

'You can't just pretend it isn't there,' said Alexander who was standing behind Claudia in the hallway with Clod, Chloe and baby Antoine.

'No, you can't,' agreed Chloe, 'not if it's determined to be there, so I think the sooner we look and get it over with, the better!'

'Yes, open the door!' said Clod.

Clarissa went to stand at the end of the hall by the library, just in case she needed to hide, and Alexander flung open the door.

'Well, it's already moved,' he announced,

looking down at the box that was now sitting right by the front door.'

'Isn't it pretty...' gasped Chloe, 'do you think we should we open it?'

'Pretty box,' cried baby Antoine, and he toddled out onto the step and lifted the lid.

'Please don't!' yelled Clarissa from the hallway, 'come back, baby!' but it was too late.

'Fireworks,' cried baby Antoine, as a cloud of blue and gold and silver and pink stars flew out of the box and danced above them with a strange buzzing sound like swarms of sparkling bees. The blue and gold swarm did a cartwheel before they disappeared into the sky, while the pink and silver swarm danced around on the step for a moment and then flew past them into the house and up the stairs.

'Can I keep the box,' asked Clod, 'after all it is empty now?'

'What a pretty box, Clodhilde,' said a voice from the stairs, 'of course you can keep it. Now I must get dinner, your Father will be home soon.'

'Mama..?' murmured Claudia, 'look, Antoine, it's our Mother.'

'Mama...' cried Clarissa, Alexander, Chloe and Clod and they all ran to kiss her.

Then the front door opened slowly and a tall, dark haired man stepped into the hall.

'I decided to come home early,' he said, 'because I suddenly realised how much I miss my family.'

'Papa…' whispered Claudia.

'Philippe!' murmured Mama, and she ran over and hugged him.

So you see it all ended happily after all.

And, just in case you're wondering, I can tell you that the wicked Marvello had enchanted Mother and Father by shutting away every bit of their happiness and joy leaving only sadness and emptiness; which was why Mother stayed in her room and Father never came home.

It was a spell that could only be broken by an even more powerful magician than Marvello, the Great Zen Xiang, and his extraordinary and wonderful Umbrella Dragon.

And, of course, by baby Antoine who wasn't afraid to open the box!

Printed in Great Britain
by Amazon